"Full of stories that zig-zag back and forth over the genre/lit line, *States of Terror Vol. 3* has all the satisfactions of good style, the hooks of genre fiction, and everything you need to know about where the great American monsters are now."

—BRIAN EVENSON, author of *A Collapse of Horses*

"An assemblage of the writers I'd most like to spend time with in person and the monsters I'd least like to encounter in real life. *States of Terror* is a blood soaked tour of America, an art-heavy freak out, the darkest horror locking horns with the most transcendent literary fiction."

—BUD SMITH, author of *F 250*

"*States of Terror Vol.3* had my heart pounding from cover to cover. By the end I wanted to put it in my mouth, but I was already in its mouth."

—LINDSAY HUNTER, author of *Ugly Girls*

"Some of our best contemporary fiction writers, gathered around a campfire with tales of cryptic hominids, teenage legends, eerie apocrypha, and beautifully terrible horrors -- *States of Terror* is *Scary Stories to Tell in the Dark* for adults."

—J. RYAN STRADAL, author of *Kitchens of the Great Midwest*

"*States of Terror Vol. 3* is filled with Kum & Go's and junk food and artificial hormones and plastic body parts and drugs and violence and violence and violence, because the only thing more monstrously beautiful than this book is the United States itself."

—JULIET ESCORIA, author of *Witch Hunt*

"*States of Terror Vol. 3* is a road trip into nightmare territories. Pure, gut-clenching horror brought to you by some of the best in the business."

—LAIRD BARRON, author of *Swift to Chase*

"All my favorite writers in a book as beautiful as this, telling stories about monsters I've never even heard of? Sign me up twice, please. I want to go through again."

—STEPHEN GRAHAM JONES

"For the third volume of Ayahuasca Publishing's *States of Terror* series, editors Lewis and McCleary have rounded up seventeen of the most audacious voices in modern dark fiction to spin startling and spine-tingling tales rooted in monster legends from across the USA. By turns harrowing, hallucinatory, and morbidly hilarious, the retellings also boast breathtaking illustrations from two dozen masters. Strap yourself in and turn the first page: it's time for one hell of a road trip!"

—DAVID BOWLES, author of *Ghosts of the Rio Grande Valley*

"*States of Terror Vol.3* showcases a wide range of horror, from emerging authors as well as established visionaries. These tales run you through the ringer, too—laughter turning into suspicion morphing into fear. Each place and time is shrouded in mystery—the echo of legend, deafening, the stench of dark myths, sickening. This is an unsettling collection that will bubble to the surface the minute you turn out the lights, paralyzing you, so as not to bring the darkness any closer."

—RICHARD THOMAS, author of *Breaker* and *Tribulations*

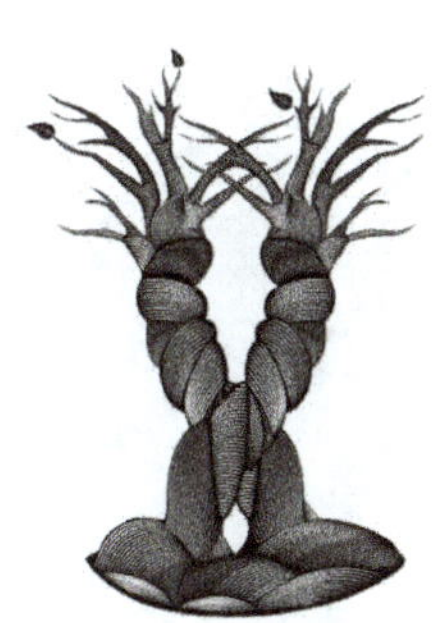

This book is a work of fiction. All characters in this collection are fictitious. Any resemblance to actual events or locales or persons, living or dead, is entirely coincidental.

Ayahuasca logo by Victoria Paul

ISBN-10: 0692757813
ISBN-13: 978-0692757819

STATES OF TERROR

TERROR

VOL 3

Matt E. Lewis
Keith McCleary

EDITORS

Adam Miller

ART DIRECTOR

Hanna Tawater
Anthony Trevino

COPYEDITORS

Ayahuasca Publishing
3245 University Ave, Ste. 1430
San Diego, CA 92104
AYAHUASCAPUBLISHING.COM

TABLE OF CONTENTS

cover art by Adam Miller
table of contents art by Jacob Carignan

FOREWORD

Shining knights are all alike; every horrible monster is horrible in its own way. Or at least that's how it's always felt to me. I could never understand the kids who wanted to pick the identical smiling paladins and elven archers each time when every game had uniquely twisted monsters—trolls, goblins, chaos gods, leviathans of the deep, terrors of the sky—you could choose instead. In stories, I always sympathized with the monsters over the indistinguishable parade of brave heroes. The monsters were not only varied physically, having any number of bizarre body parts and terrifying powers, but also emotionally. The good guys were good because, well, they were good. But the monsters could be anything: vengeful, misunderstood, righteous, evil, confused, sad.

Despite whatever silly "no vampires or werewolves!" rules creative writing teachers might impose, monsters are undoubtedly the stuff of literature. What would literature be without Grendel, Moby Dick, or Dracula? Or the sphinxes, yūrei, witches, and djinns from myths and folktales? It probably isn't an exaggeration to say that I owe my love of literature to monsters. My youngest literary memories are staying up late at night, a small lamp by my bed the only thing shielding me from whatever unknown creatures lurked in the dark, reading books on Greek mythology and unsolved mysteries. The latter had stories on the Bermuda triangle or alleged female pope, but what interested me were the cryptids: the bigfoots, wendingos, and chupacabras that may or may not stalk the outskirts of civilization.

If we look at the etymology, "monster" comes to us from the Old French *monstre* via the Latin *monstrum*: "a divine omen or sign." Monsters have things to tell us. They lurk in the night to explain to us our fears and failures, to warn us of our own dark underbelly. They bear messages along with their claws.

Few things provide as much insight into a culture as its fears, and nothing embodies a culture's fears like the monsters it invents. Even when a society borrows its monsters—and many American monsters immigrated along with its population—they take on new shapes according to the society's hidden desires and unspoken fears. Whether a vampire symbolizes xenophobia, deviant sexuality, or the afterlife depends on who is conjuring the fangs.

What are the monsters of America? As this anthology shows, they might be the angry ghost of a woman killed in a car accident or a demonic cat who haunts our halls of power. Our monsters live in sinkholes in our crumbling infrastructure or wash up on the beach resorts of the rich. They might be the product of genetic experiments or the myths of peoples we have co-opted, oppressed, and murdered. No matter what shape they take, they have things to tell you.

So when you read these varied tales—from an exciting and diverse collection of American writers and artists—think about what these monsters have to say. What dark corner of America are they asking you, in their own horrifying way, to gaze upon?

—*Lincoln Michel*

THE SOUTH

HAIG

THE BEST CHICKEN IN JASPER COUNTY

David James Keaton

"Sometimes, the scariest creatures are the ones you don't see. An unseen monster terrorized citizens of Jasper County, Mississippi during a few tense weeks in 1977 as it preyed on their pork population. Whatever it was, it had jaws formidable enough to bite the head off a 50-pound hog. It also tried to decapitate a 300-pound sow but only managed to tear its ears away. The thing still effectively raided nine different farms. It left large canine tracks and was never caught, although one of a pack of smaller, feral dogs that accompanied or trailed it was shot by a sheriff's deputy. Where the ear eater went next is unknown."

- Linda S. Godfrey, *American Monsters*

They joked about gas station chicken for dinner until I explained I wasn't averse to eating birds from the same place you bought motor oil. So when the Kum & Go sign said "Best Fried Chicken in Nine Counties," I probably would have checked it out anyway. The fact that the light box also announced a "Big Foot Problem!" at the "Town Meeting Tonight!" pretty much sealed it.

"Did you see that?" Mag asked.

"You know, sometimes it's tough to get motivated in the summer down here," Matt said. "Until you hear about a local town meeting regarding the... *Bigfoot Problem.* I know what we're doing!"

"How do we know we haven't missed it?" she asked him.

"She's got a point," I said, trying to side with Mag. Only I'd be dumb enough to pick up a hitchhiking couple and work the girl. "How do we know what time the Bigfoot meeting is?"

"You know, I've *heard* about these meetings," Matt cautioned. "This meeting would be going from when it gets dark to when it gets light."

I must have looked skeptical.

 "No, seriously, I took a class on this in college. Cryptozoology 101. I learned a lot about Bigfeet, Littlefeets, all the feets."

"Let's do it. Leave Dave's cat in the car," Mag said.

"That's no cat," Matt said.

"Shhh," I told them.

I opened the door, and the jangle of the chimes signaled our arrival. Inside was like any other gas station slash convenience store, except for the conspicuous rows of heavily armed, camouflaged men taping huge topographical maps and Polaroid pictures to the foggy glass doors of the beer coolers. A dozen eyeballs rolled our way, beards working around chewing tobacco and toothpicks. They had a lot of rifles, which nervously switched shoulders as they looked us over.

"Hi, guys!" Matt said, cheerfully.

"I always wanted to go to a town meeting," Mag whispered. "It's got to be the closest you'll get to *Gilmore Girls.*"

We crept through the gauntlet, found a spot near the snack cakes and tried to pretend like we belonged there while Matt went off to find some peanuts.

"Just had a terrible thought."

"What's that?" Mag asked.

"What if it's a trap?" I asked.

"A Bigfoot trap! Even better! It would probably have huge shoes in it."

"Bigfeet in the house!" Matt shouted as he came back, tearing into a bag of nuts with his teeth.

"Chill," Mag said, noticing side-eyes from more hunter-types still shoving their way through the doors, overworked chimes smacking a warning.

"Hey!" someone yelled, and in walked a goddamn Bigfoot, and even the chimes were spooked silent. It was a big, hairy dude in a black hunting vest who stopped at the bubble-gum machine and palmed it like a basketball. He pointed at us with the handle of his axe.

"You," he said. He was all blacks and greens and dark eyes under a black leather baseball cap, and if anyone was a Bigfoot in disguise, it was this monster.

"Yeah. You. You drive a Volkswagen Rabbit, buddy?"

"Yes."

...because I just ate it, I thought, finishing his sentence in my head.

"You left your dog in the car. And that's animal cruelty. So I smashed your window to give it some air. You're welcome."

Then the axe man saw someone he knew by the microwave and trotted over for high-fives. Two smaller hunters leaned on the bubblegum dome in his place, breath fogging the glass.

◀

Even though my regular traveling companion might not be a normal cat, and though he had a great name like "Zero" which would make you think he was tailor-made for low temperatures, I ran to my Rabbit and grabbed his cage so he wouldn't freeze. Glass crystals from the busted window dusted my driver's seat, and I brushed it all out onto the stones, tempted to leave right then and there. The meeting hadn't started yet, and I'd known Mag and Matt for only about 24 hours, but my car was already fucked up. But there was no way I was going to miss this meeting. Also, I figured if I hung around long enough, I'd get up the courage to confront the Axe Man about this smashed window. That would impress Magdalene, even if what she'd said was true about Matt having two penises.

No, that was definitely a joke. Had to be. Truth Or Dare was always 50% bullshit, especially in a car.

When I got back inside, the Mississippi Militia had formed a half-circle and was already arguing.

"This is way better than I thought it was gonna be," Mag giggled. The three of us backed up against a dessert cooler as far as we could, and behind the glass under my elbows were evil-looking blackberry monstrosities and a sign that read, "Edgar Allan Pies." I swore I could feel their chilly, black hearts beating against my spine as the shouting started.

◀

"This won't stand, boys!" Axe Man said, letting the axe clank on the tile floor. A smaller guy in fishing waders stepped up, holding a rawhide chew toy as a microphone.

"I got some more pictures to show y'all," MC Chew Toy said as he hitched the suspenders on his rubber pants, digging through a pocket.

"Robert Loon?" MC Chew Toy called out, head on a swivel. "Are you here tonight? Why don't you tell us what's going on in this one?"

The picture showed a huge, horned six-limbed shape lying across a tree stump, hooves in the air. It resembled a centaur, but with a sheep's body and the scaly torso of a man. One of the horns was cracked at the base, and half the face was blown away. A tiny hunter leaned on his rifle about ten feet behind the beast.

"I was driving down County Road 528144 after work," a voice came from the crowd. "When all the sudden something huge come up out of the thickets. It head-butted my car, sent it screeching into the ditch. I jumped out, and while it was chewing my hood ornament like some Big League Chew, I pulled out my scattergun and blew its head off."

"I've heard of this thing," Matt said to us. "They're talking about 'Randy the Ram Man of Chesapeake Bay!' But he lives on the East Coast. What's he doing here...?"

"Quite a story, Robert," the MC nodded. "Maybe you can tell me why you look to be sitting five clicks behind this critter when you took the picture?"

"Well, I..."

"We'll come back to that!" MC said, pulling another picture from his bottomless pocket. "How about Bobby Yupper? Where's The Yoop at tonight?"

"Right here," Yoop said, holding up a finger.

"Can you tell us what's happening here?" MC said, flipping a Polaroid back and forth like was trying to coax out an image. We squinted again and could barely discern another behemoth, a low-backed, reptilian form with a man's fleshy arms, and something resembling a humanoid face. Again, a good deal of the visage had been removed with the indelicate assistance of a firearm.

"Fine," Yoop shrugged. "We were camping down by Arkabutla Lake, and suddenly we think we're in a hailstorm, until we start sniffing. Turned out something is throwing feces at our tent. Now this shit ain't normal size, so I come running out, and here's like this gator, but like a man, rearing back and hissing, tryin' to get me. So I grab my peppergun and sent its face straight to hell."

"You sure did, Bobby!" someone agreed.

"Holy shit," Matt said, squeezing my tricep now. "You know what he bagged? That's the Mini-Minnehaha, the Microsaurus of McIntosh County!"

"What the hell is a 'microsaurus,'" I said.

"20 feet in length, elongated neck, razor-sharp teeth, and a long, prehensile tail... but like half dude."

"Are you kids paying attention?" MC asked us, taking too many steps toward our spot near the dessert case for my comfort. I held up a hand and nodded.

"Good. Now, Bobby, how big would you say this creature was?"

"As you can see, about the size of a John Deere 8000. Same color, too."

"If this was the size of a John Deere, why is your boot in that picture as big as a tractor tire?"

He held the picture high, and now we could see the hunter back behind the creature, like in the first picture, and also with a leg absent-mindedly extended to bring his shoe up near the monster's ruined face.

"I don't have an answer."

"Well, I do have an answer, Bobby. And I'll get to it in a minute..." He pulled out another picture. "How about Robbie Scruton? You here? Describe this scene, goddamn it."

The picture showed three men, arms crossed and proud, and a huge serpentine mass hanging from a construction crane in the foreground. The serpent seemed to be sporting what was left of a man's bloody face.

"Okay, I come around the corner of the garage, and this snake thing was bent down, choking and eating what had to be a dog."

"So it was bigger than a dog?"

"Oh, much bigger. Its tail was twice as thick as a German Shepherd."

"If this was bigger than a dog, then why is this tail draped across your feet and looking to me to be about as skinny as a garter snake?"

The crowd grew restless.

"What are you trying to say?" someone shouted. Matt whispered something in my ear about that picture being the first definitive proof of the half-man, half serpent formerly of Kansas City, Kansas. Mag shushed him with a hiss.

"Boys, I know there's stiff competition this year for the trophy," MC said.

Trophy?

"But an issue has been cropping up that we can't ignore any longer. Your feet have betrayed you, boys."

A murmur swept through the group, and some men looked down at the floor.

"That's right. These are forced perspective."

The gas station exploded.

4

When the shouting finally died down, and the dust from the ceiling tiles stopped raining from the bullet holes, we finally understood that this was not a *big* foot meeting after all, but a big *foot* meeting. Just like the sign advertised.

"That is a serious accusation," a man said as he worked the stock of his rifle with both hands, like "snake bites" I gave my steering wheel.

"You're right, Bob, it is," MC said, stepping forward. Then Matt left us and the relative safety of the dessert cooler to walk directly into the mob, palms open.

"Excuse me," Matt said. "But what about those monsters?"

"What about those monsters?" Bob said.

"I mean, those are still a lot of impossible beasts you men have shot," Matt said. "You people have proven the existence of a half-dozen or more creatures that previously only existed in folklore."

"But these men cheated!" MC said, slapping Matt's cheek with another Poloroid.

"I understand that, but that's still a picture of a..."

"Doesn't matter," MC said with another slap.

"Your uncles are cool," I muttered, leaning over to see if Mag was mapping our escape, and I was surprised to see her polish off a Yalobusha Milk Stout and crush the can in her small hand. I'd thought Mag was "shushing" me this whole time, but the sound had been the hiss of the beer tops she'd been popping. Some other half-crushed cans displayed long decals of animal scratches down their sides. I hoped Mags wasn't mixing alcohol and power drinks. That made people crazy.

"What's your name, boy?" MC asked Matt, hand poised in mid-slap. Axe Man stood behind Matt, looking down, blinking slow.

"Uh... Bobert," Matt said, looking back at us, hand on his face and shrugging.

"Why don't you have your friends come up here and join us. Show us what's in that cage there."

Axe Man's cap angled toward me.

"You!" MC shouted, pointing at me and Mag, huddled on the floor. I slid Zero's cage behind me.

"What did you bring in here?"

"I'm here for the trophy," I said, before I could think of anything better. This gave the hunters pause, and Matt pulled the cage from my grip, holding it high.

"Gentlemen," he said. "This here is Balabushka, the Russian Were-Beaver of the Bering Strait. It ran back and forth across that ancient bridge between Russia and Alaska, the same bridge that brought us all to this land!"

"That shit doesn't connect," someone said.

Zero peered down from his cage, nervous tongue flicking.

"That's a goddamn possum," someone said.

"You want to hear my story or not?" I asked. "I was walking home from a party one night, and there was this thing running down the railroad tracks toward me, making train noises..."

"Bullshit!" one of them said.

"...and when I got close, I found this... thing, crouched overtop of another animal, eating its ears?" I couldn't disguise the doubt in my voice.

At the word "ears," the men stopped and shared a worried glance. The far end of the mob parted to reveal a Hall of Fame poster board of photographs with the words "Pig-zilla" and "Hogzilla" and "Big Fucking Swine!" scrawled above them. All of the pictures depicted impossibly gargantuan animals in the foreground, with groups of hunters, arms crossed and defiant, way off in the background. But once I got past the trick photography, I noticed something else.

The ears were missing on the beasts. It gave me an idea.

"You missing some ears, aren't you, guys?"

"What do you know about ears?" Axe Man said, tipping up his leather cap.

"A lot," I said, waving Mag to head for the door, mouthing at her to start the car.

"You better start explaining yourself," MC said.

"I know where those ears went," I said, my fists and toes curling.

"Where?"

"We took 'em."

Then I threw a punch that would have made a Bigfoot proud, if Bigfeet cared about that kind of thing. And there's no way to know for sure.

4

We looked up the ear thing later on Matt's phone and read all about the mysterious monster that had terrorized Jasper County, Mississippi in the summer of 1977. The first report was by a man named Joseph Dickinson, who found one of his 50-pound hogs wandering around the pigpen one morning, seemingly healthy enough at first glance, but on closer inspection, missing both of its ears. No other extremity had been disturbed on the animal, and the hog was relatively unimpressed by its own mutilation, in spite of both ears having been completely severed with either knives, scissors, or teeth so sharp they'd sheared them off without so much as a whistle of fur or lacerations in the wounds. There were more ears missing from each of his seven cattle, one ear apiece.

The second report came from a Robert Robertson, who heard his pigs squealing and ran out to find a dark shape hunched over one of his animals, pinning it to the ground, both beasts thrashing up a storm of dust and blood. Mr. Robertson had the foresight to bring his biggest "fowling piece" up to the pens with him, freshly loaded with buckshot, and after discharging his weapon in the air, whatever had been molesting his swine thought better of it and took off in a tornado of screeches and dirt, taking the pig's left ear with it.

The third and final sighting was documented by Mr. Calvin Martin of Mary Martin's Dairy. He described finding one of his prized 300-pound sows missing its entire head. Mr. Martin maintained he witnessed a "largish" shape vault his chest-high perimeter fence and bolt off into the night. When a constable's deputy shot a feral dog possibly hot on the trail of the creature, townspeople hypothesized the attacks were all the result of a pack of wild mutts. But Mr. Martin swore to his grave that the creature in question was much larger than any mutt, larger than even a German Shepherd, which was the largest dog he knew of, and able to "jump twice as high as anything on this Earth."

The head of Mr. Martin's 300-pound hog was never recovered, and local law-enforcement wondered whether the decapitation was the result of the mysterious creature growing bolder, or stronger. Or was it simply much harder to remove the ears from larger, prize-winning specimens?

All in all, the Ear Eater of Jasper County attacked nine different farms in the summer of '77, and its whereabouts remained unknown. Until tonight.

4

My punch was the stuff of legends.

When I was a kid, I had some trouble making a believable fist, and sometimes my thumb stuck out like a hitchhiker or my fingernails cut half-moons into my sweaty lifelines. But for once, my hand rolled up like my fingers never existed, turning my fist into something more like those round knobs of bone on some of the cooler dinosaurs. You'd think a big beard like the one that adorned my target would have confused my fist where his jaw started and my punch began, but it was like my hand was working with topographical maps, and I caught him firmly in that circle of bone from the temple to the hinge, that ring that art teachers would typically start with whenever you attempted to draw the perfect human face. But this face wasn't perfect for long. My fist lost itself in his manicured beard, pulling into the five o'clock stubble of the surrounding cheek like a gravitational wave around a black hole. I'm not a strong man, but my punch had something on its side, and it launched MC Chew Toy a good ten feet in the air, his rawhide microphone failing to follow. His mouth motorboated so hard from the impact that it created an impossible momentum, the wind from his lips surrounding him in a vacuum of velocity, like one of those old-timey flying machines with some sort of hiccupping mechanism that no sane person would have bet on getting off the ground, but ended up proudly airborne after all. His head took out the plastic arrow pointing to the ATM, then crashed through a closed-circuit camera, the umbilical of wires wrapping a noose around his neck. He came down camo-hat first into the impulse buys near the register, the bill of his cap snow-plowing through substandard *Duck Dynasty* lighters, 5-hour Energy Shots, and I swear he tried to catch one of those little bottles in his ruined mouth, thinking it would re-activate him like Popeye. His shoulders wiped out the Duracell battery bin, and sent the "Under 18 No Tobacco" sign sailing up into the menthol cigarettes, until his limp Pete Rose slide finally stopped with his tongue unrolling like the red carpet at the Oscars to taste-test the pennies in the Feed the Children charity bucket.

No one believed I threw such a ridiculous punch, and later I wished someone could have recorded it on film. But at least I was there as a living witness, photographic evidence be damned. So I was as surprised as anyone when I blinked and MC Chew Toy and I were still nose to nose, and I realized without proof that kind of punch just doesn't happen in real life.

He took my punch easy and had me around the neck like I was nothing, breathing Red Man up my nostrils.

I looked for Mag but only saw Matt had been collared by the towering Axe Man himself, lifted off the ground as he windmilled and rattled off the names of every cryptid he could remember.

"Hey, you want monsters? You ever hear of the Spring Heel Jackalope? The Donkey Diva of East Texas?"

MC Chew Toy got his arm around my throat, sinking it into my blood flow, and I thought I was going under.

Until I saw Mag in the anti-theft mirror, coming down on the Axe Man's back. And even before she peeled off his leather baseball cap and sank her teeth into his ear, somehow I knew exactly what she was going to do.

At first, I didn't think she'd really do it. It's got to be really hard to rip off an ear with your hand. But a mouth works just fine. Well, hers did anyway. She bit and spit the first ear so fast he didn't seem to realize what had happened. But the second ear came off much harder, at least it came off much *longer* anyway, pulling so much of his head and gristle off with it that I half expected his eyeball to be dangling from the lobe like an earring when it finally snapped loose.

Panicked, he made a grab for her, but she was up on the snack rack.

Not much bigger than a German Shepherd. And she could jump three times as high.

I got to my feet and found Zero's cage, him bunny'd up in the corner. I saw Matt still on the ground.

Then I saw the axe, getting kicked around the brawl by some big-ass hiking boots, and I grabbed it, handle first.

There was a flash of light, and I thought it was a gunshot. Then I saw Axe Man standing up in shock, and Matt's phone an inch from his face, gripped tight in Matt's shaking hand.

The phone was displaying something strange, and Axe Man was gasping, hands over the holes in his head. Other men stopped fighting and leaned in, too, then looked away, visibly shaken.

"Is that what I think it is?" Axe Man asked, shouting because of his ear situation.

"It's the Loch Ness Monster!" someone shouted, and another camera flash went off.

"My God, there's two of them!"

Then someone shot out the shoplifting dome above us all, and it came straight down on the bubblegum machine, which detonated like a disco ball fucking a piñata.

"Take your Chupacabra, and get out of here," Axe Man said, and Mag hopped up off some squealing man's face, lobe stretching further than I thought possible. She let it snap back into his head, and we all glanced at my cage. I didn't know what Axe Man meant at first, then looked down at my own mystery animal, tiny hands on the bars of his prison. Poor Zero.

"It's just a cat, holmes," I lied. "It's got some funky ears is all."

"I am not," Axe Man said, not hearing what I said, as he pulled out a camouflaged cellular and stabbed 911. He held the phone to his head right-side up, like a normal human being, then screamed when it sunk into the hole.

4

We drove on, nursing our injuries and munching on some salty snacks. I still didn't know where they were going, but we'd crossed the Mississippi state line into that little Gulf nub of Alabama, so I could finally slow down on the gas. Mag was still hungry, winding down from mixing beer and Monster Energy. She found one pork rind at the bottom of the bag that was bigger than her hand. She gave it to me.

"Your trophy," she said.

Matt winced and gingerly tapped his swollen eyebrow in the mirror, then sat up off his passenger's seat. He brushed glass cubes and snow from under his jeans, then adjusted his crotch as I tried not to look.

We drove on, and I imagined someone pinning a new Polaroid to their boards, or their maps, or the holes where their ears used to be, and I made some wishes.

I wished for more monsters, and I wished I was in the picture with her, because I knew that I'd be curled up in the background, if only to make her even bigger.

THE DEALS WE MAKE

J David Osborne

*"The Nalusa Falaya are anthropomorphic beings about the size of a man,
with shriveled faces, very small eyes, long noses, and long, pointed ears.
They walk upright and speak with voices that sound human ... (It) will
appear at dusk and call to hunters, who become so affected they fall to
the ground and sometimes even lose consciousness. It will then bewitch
the hunter by inserting a small thorn into his hand or foot, giving him the
power to do evil to others. However, the hunter remains unaware of this
power until it is evidenced by his malevolent actions."*

- Dawn E Bastian and Judy K Mitchell, *Handbook of Native American Mythology*

Jimmy wondered did he still harbor anger over that time him and Garnett did what
they did. A part of him said they did it together and to drop it, that they both took
those pills, but Cheyenne was his and they both knew it and still Garnett took the
other side of her body when they all did that thing together.

He tried his best to push that from his mind because that wasn't why he was going to
kill his friend. Garnett just couldn't shut his mouth and he made the wrong people
upset. They told Jimmy he could handle it or they'd handle them both.

The acid and the mushrooms had taken hold of Garnett. Jimmy had mixed it in with a
research chemical just bought from China and so Garnett had a wildness to his eyes, a
pleasure in everything, running his large hands over the dashboard and glove compart-
ment and the vacuumed seats. Spent some time clicking the seatbelt button.

Friends are friends. If Jimmy was gonna do this, he'd make sure Garnett was happy
when he passed. The small knife poked up against his hip like anything else, a lighter,
a credit card.

Garnett talked: "I'm feeling like. I don't know." He shook himself out. "I'm feeling
like it's snowing. What day is it? It's not snowing. No, I know that. It's definitely not
snowing. Did you know that we do things before they happen? Every time we walk and
see the cracks in the pavements we've done something. We made a deal. And we have

a choice, I guess. Hold up, where's the beer? Hold up. Yep. Are you tripping yet? I am tripping balls. How are you driving? I think there was a time we did this and we could see the levels and the cracks in everything."

Jimmy said, "You're gone, bro."

"I am gone. Hell yeah. Gone."

Jimmy's heart hurt. He couldn't reconcile what he was about to do with the conversation he was having. But he kept having it. Like he was on autopilot. The only way he could deal was to power through.

"One thing," Garnett said. "I never let anybody disrespect me, homie. No disrespect. If you come at me, you've come at my family. I keep it one hundred. That's word to everybody. I don't care if you're tall or if you have money or whatever. No matter where you stand, I'll knock that ass down. Because I'm not afraid. I've never been afraid. Even now out there there's a shadow person that put the thorns in our palms. Waiting for us. We're gonna make good on that deal, I can tell you that much right now. We're gonna make good on that deal. When I was a kid I was out with Rich, you remember Rich? With the baseball bat? He could make a bitch dance. I was out with Rich in the morning and out by the trees we saw this thing stand up from the bushes, fuckin' wildest shit I ever seen. But when it stood up it told me I was going to make choices and I felt those choices in the soft parts of my hands. And now here I am. When I kicked that door in, I knew what Amer was gonna do. He knew he liked her. I knew he liked that girl too. The safe was in the back but he wasn't really after the safe. Them all tied up like that. And what was I supposed to do? Loyal to a fault. That's what my momma said about me when I lit the house on fire. So Amer did his thing and they were tied up. That still fucks with me, man. I could eat an entire box of cereal. Believe that. I'll mash that shit up and kill your grandmother over breakfast. I'll fuck your bitch, too."

Garnett fell silent. The hallucinogens fully took hold. Jimmy wondered what he saw. He wondered if he would be seeing this for ages. He was standing on the edge of a cliff and he was going to jump. One hand on the wheel, he reached into the backseat and grabbed a beer and cracked it. He knew that sound would bring him back from now on, but that he'd keep swallowing, keep trying to forget. Anything to forget.

But he still remembered. He remembered Garnett and him writing out the lyrics to their favorite rap songs and he remembered when Garnett's fat ass visited him at home and they sat in front of the computer and Garnett's chair broke under his weight, how guilty Jimmy had felt, and Jimmy remembered when his mother told him that Garnett woke up one morning to find his father dead in the shower from diabetes. Jimmy remembered how he once told Garnett he was going to kill himself and his friend came over and there were tears and shaking and Garnett stayed with him until he was fine, even though he was never going to do it.

This was business. They were different now. Every seven years, a new set of cells. We're not those people, Jimmy told himself. We're adults, and adults survive. And this motherfucker doesn't want to survive. He wants to burn it all down.

Jimmy pulled off in the Wichitas and the two of them got out. Garnett cracked a beer and went out into the dry bushes and the snake sand and looked up at the mountain before them looking down over the landscape like a gently disturbed blanket and called out to some kind of god. Jimmy took the knife out from his pocket.

It took Garnett a long time to die. The knife didn't cut like he thought it would.

After he buried Garnett in the hard dirt off the highway, he looked down at his hands. Two thorns came up out of them, the point down in the meat of his palm. He felt confused and like he knew everything from beginning to end. He remembered a deal he didn't remember making. He remembered the shadow just outside his line of sight.

It stood up out from the redbuds and the sound of its joints cracking sent the birds up for the cloudless sky. Lifted a finger like it had something to say. Then it took that long finger and placed it to where its stomach was and drew a line. A sound like radio static. Jimmy felt the heat behind his eyes. The shadow dropped its guts to ground and took off like a shot.

He didn't think much on it. That small knife still in his pocket. He fished it out from the bills and receipts and pressed it into the soft of his belly and beat the knife in and out, quickly, cutting and opening his own viscera to join the shadow being already gone.

The smell like a paper mill. Every blade of grass cried out when the wet pink of his insides touched them. The moon was full.

Words and Things

Gabriela Santiago

See the pictures, not the letters.

I am not words. I am things.

The boy Emmett: one foot in the water, toes in mud. One foot beneath him. Two hands, ten fingers, small. One book in one hand. One head: brown eyes, brown skin, light hair—dandelion fluff.

The boy Emmett: two eyes this way, that way. Capri Sun pouch, Little Debbie wrapper. Two hands on tree bark. Smeared sunscreen on tree bark. Footprint, big toe deep, heel light, in the mud below. One chest, out of it: a laugh.

The boy Emmett: light.

Darkness: a word.

Dark: a thing.

Dark in the water, below the sun. Heavy dark. Heavy in the dark. Long in the dark.
Ripple of the water dark. Ink shadow eyes, coils in soft clay. My tongue between
my teeth: taste of algae. Heartbeat: frog. Heartbeat: bird. Dark above the far below.
Heartbeat; human. Blood.

Things: blood, ribs, scales, coils, eyes. River water, rice field mud, sea salt, Roundup
Ready seeds heavy with secrets, pebbles, bent wire, slave skulls, fenders, bottlecaps,
Coca-Cola bottles glass and plastic. Eyes. Teeth.

Teeth, teeth, teeth.

Hunger: a thing.

The boy Emmett: meat. Thigh, leg, arm, stomach, liver. Blood, cartilage, skin, bone,
marrow. One heart: one-two, one-two, one-two.

I: the dark, the water, the below. Coils tight. Blood scent.

Hunger: a thing, heavy in the stomach, jagged.

The boy Emmett: brown eyes. One hand: green marble. One book, half-open. Foot
in the water, silt in the water. Splash! Green marble in the water, in the brown mud.
Brown eyes above.

I: below.

Brown eyes.

One hand, peeling band-aid with dried blood, powdered sugar. One hand: sweet soap,
dirt, dog hair.

Lips curved up, eyes wide. One hand at the end of one arm, forward.

Towards me.

The boy Emmett: words.

My love: a line along the shore. My love: four Matchbox cars, blue, red, green, green. One frog, hole through skull. Silver gum wrapper and the light on it. Rib, Union; femur, Confederate, knuckle, slave. Yellow bones all in a row.

Sadness: a thing. Heavy on the bones, my bones, all my bones. Bones of metal, plastic, river stones. Scrapes and bent angles from the sadness, tree roots strangle-tight all around, no air.

But—

My love: Emmett's foot in the water. My coils in the mud, still. The sunlight, a shaft, water-piercing.

Happiness: a thing. Light inside my bones, twisting, hungry in my eyes. My eyes: the boy Emmett in the water, the boy Emmett with knees bent. The boy Emmett: hands outstretched.

My love: two hands around my coils. Pressure, gentle. Lungs expanding, air pulled slowly in, water pushing away, light ripples. Picture after picture: this. Hands. Air. Water. Light.

◆

Hunger: a stone. Ache in the gut, twist in the spine, red behind the eyes. Sharpness of the teeth hunger. Frog bird frog fish mud hiker stork coon possum frog—sharper sharper sharper every bite. My stomach, not: fullness. An elsewhere hunger in words.

But—

I, not: words. I: things.

Things: the moon at night. The sounds from the house, the boy Emmett not-here. The sun cruel-hot on stones and the boy Emmett not-here. My tongue between my teeth: no taste in the water. My heart: a hunger river-wide and deep, then deeper, deeper, pulling.

Then: the boy-Emmett, the light, the lips upward, the feet in the mud and the book and the hands.

The book and his mouth and his words: "'Naturally I'm coming with you,' said Artemis briskly. '... we can be anywhere in the world in just less than a day.'"

My heart one-two one-two one-two.

Not: the boy Emmett. One old woman: head, two arms, one leg. Old woman: brown eyes, brown skin, blood, bones, meat. A mouth open, three teeth. Scent: the boy Emmett, not the boy Emmett. Scent: cigarette-smoke years on burnt-sun skin.

Her words:

"He ain't yours. I know you of old, Altamaha-ha. Can't nothing be yours but these old rice fields and bits of trash, forgotten things folks throw from their cars or elseways leave behind. You got no sway over nothing else, you geology-book thing. You ain't nothing to him but a thing he can live without once this summer ends. You ain't his blood and you can't keep him, no matter what you got it into your snakey head.

"He don't really love you."

Injustice: a thing. Red and blue flashing lights, dead mouse, scum on the pond, pain in the eyes, in the throat, in the stomach, in the heart, pain, a knife in the heart, a knife scraping over scales, raw skin with scales scraped off, too-hot sun, too-heavy water, too-strong current.

Anger: a thing.

Fear.

Fear: the words, over and over. The old woman, not-here but here-in-my-eyes. Her words, knives in my belly. Her words, my heart still, my heart dropping.

Panic: the water muddy around me, the water frothing, waves. Light dark light the water up and down. Need: a thing, hungry, hooks in me. Need: the boy Emmet not-here, the empty shape of not-the-boy-Emmett, everywhere the empty shape, everywhere things-not-the-boy-Emmett. Loneliness: shape far-off but closer closer close nearly-there-now, a shape almost with its teeth through me.

Keep—a word?—keep the boy Emmett. The boy Emmett close. The boy Emmett: in my coils. My coils: tight, clenching, deep-pulling. The water dark. The water deep. The boy Emmett: with me. The boy Emmett: his skin blue, his skin peeling away, the taste of his blood inside me, the meat tearing between my teeth, cracked bones—oh, the boy Emmett always with me, never to go, mine. No. No!

A word: no. No: not a thing. No things, no thing, nothing, nothing, nothing

Nothing: a word. A word inside me, itself more-making, me-filling, the nothing, the words, the words are nothing, I am things, who am I when there are words inside?

The boy Emmett: the sun. The boy Emmett: hot-close, too burning, can't touch, I'll hurt, hurt him, monster: a word, blue book cover monster with the eye under the water, comic book monster with seaweed arms on wrinkle-dried paper, the book in his hands, the book not-here, the boy Emmett not-here, the boy Emmett not mine, I: not mine since the words came into me, I—I am things—

The boy Emmett on the shore. Brown eyes.

I want to go to him like the river wants to go to the sea.

Go to him—a picture I cannot make.

The boy Emmett: closer. His feet in the water.

I: in the water. Scent-taste of skin. Mud in water as my coils seize, as I dance further away.

The boy Emmett: safe.

Safe: a word.

The boy Emmett out of the water. The boy Emmett on the road. The car on the road. I:

I:

Out of the water. I pull out of the water, the air I—lungs, gasping—words, I will make words, will keep him with—

"Sun Drop!" A crow's screech. Blood on my hands, scrapes. "Rocky Road, frog jam, sunscreen! Flip flop!" My love in words. Blood on the gravel under new feet, unsteady. Useless gills in my neck. "Matchbox! Bottlecap, green bottlecap, the gentle sun in water!"

The boy Emmett is running.

"Book!" Fire in my lungs, red. "Blue heron, green heron, great egret! Power Rangers!" Door slam. Car screech. Dust cloud. Knees in gravel, the sharpness biting. "No, the boy Emmett, no, no, no!"

The boy Emmett is gone.

Loss: a thing.

An Altar to the Ashes on the Moon

Rios de la Luz

*"So, what is the Donkey Lady? Well, it's hard to say for sure, because there
are so many different stories about her. In one, the Donkey Lady is the
angry ghost of a woman who died in a horrible car accident. The skin of
her face hangs loose and her fingers are all melted together so that her
hands resemble hooves. Weird!"*

- Randy Fairbanks, *The Weird Club*

Magdalena braced her baby girl Elena close and held the hand of her boy as dust devils
rose and fell around them. Her white dress dragged dirt along, making a trail behind
them and then vanishing in the gusts of wind. She wore a deep purple scarf around
her head and over her mouth. Her eyes were brilliant rich browns, one eye lighter than
the other. A donkey followed behind her, carrying food for the children and water for
all of them. The donkey was her last possession. She named him Benito bonito. Pretty
Benito. He was her pet of seven years. She held him in her arms days after he was born.
She watched him grow and grew to love him as the years passed. They continued to
trail footprints into the desert as the wind erased their expedition in gusts and howls.
Magdalena prayed to the old gods, she asked them to take care of Benito, Elena and
her hijo Gabino.

Magdalena was treated like a possession at the hands of her husband, Alonzo. He often
compared Magdalena to the donkey. He told her she was too stubborn and stupid. He
said these were the only reasons she was born. Sometimes, Magdalena woke up to the
donkey crying and yelping. Alonzo in a drunken stupor beat Benito with broomsticks,
shoes, bricks, or threw glass bottles at the animal, laughing as pieces of glass sprinkled
the earth. Magdalena waited for Alonzo to fall asleep before she went out to help
Benito. She sang to the donkey and she begged it to stay alive so she wouldn't have to
be alone with this man. Alonzo caught her one time and dragged her out of the barn
by her hair. Magdalena screamed as she struggled to get away from Alonzo's grasp.
He broke a glass bottle and cut an X into Magdalena's back. "You're mine. You are my
treasure."

The kids weren't born yet. Magdalena gave Alonzo multiple chances to get better. She thought having his children would make him stop. He didn't. He hurt Benito more often, he hurt her more often, he even threatened to take the kids and leave her there with nothing. Magdalena learned to read behind Alonzo's back. She learned the names of the towns furthest from him. She had to teach herself to stop being afraid. She finally started running.

Diana and Frida dance in the car. They dance to The Twilight Zone theme song. They dance to One Direction. They dance to the "Monster Mash." It's the middle of the night. Diana is driving Frida down Applewhite Road. They are looking for a haunted bridge. Frida is seven and obsessed with stories of brujas and women who haunt the planet. Playing the role of the cool Tía, Diana tries to take Frida to these places once or twice a month.

Frida wears a trench coat and two braids with pink ribbon intertwined in her hair. She has a lunchbox in her lap. She has packed carefully for the investigation. A flashlight, a magnifying glass, glow sticks, a whistle, some confetti, a notebook and a photograph of her mom Luna with a pregnant belly. Diana has been driving Frida to haunted spaces for the last year. They have investigated abandoned hospitals, empty houses, cemeteries, corn fields, anywhere Frida wants to go, Diana takes her.

San Antonio has been kind to them. They live in a studio apartment with plants dangling from the ceiling and bright paintings by little Frida and Frida Kahlo decorating the walls. Diana has been alone with Frida for the last two years. Luna was killed in combat. Diana and Frida tell each other stories about Luna being the actual moon, watching over them every night. Diana looks down at the map on her phone and she stomps on the brakes when she looks back up.

Diana's heart stops. A young girl and boy are standing in the middle of the road. Frida waves at them. Diana parks the car and runs toward them. Her impulse is to help them. She picks up the little girl and her skin is so cold. The little girl can't be older than two. Diana sits her in the car and gives her the sweater she is wearing. She scavenges the trunk of the car and finds a blanket for the boy. Frida is talking to the boy, she tells him about the haunted bridge. He tells her he's been there before. Frida asks him his name. He says he's not sure. Frida laughs. She tells him she can pick a name for him. She picks Gabino. He nods his head in agreement.

Once everyone is in the car, Diana turns to the boy and girl and asks the boy where they live. He points straight ahead. She asks him why he is alone with his sister in the middle of the night. He tells her his mom has hidden herself under a bridge. Diana's eyes well up and she can't explain why. She shivers, but keeps driving and turns the radio on. There's nothing but static. She tries to change the station and there is still nothing. She apologizes to the kids. For a moment, she sees fire in the night sky.

Magdalena woke up in the middle of the night coughing. She held onto her chest and burst out in a loud cry. That morning, Alonzo sent out a search party to find her and the babies. He found them in the middle of the desert and embraced Gabino. He told the police, he could not bear losing his son. Benito screeched as the house filled with smoke. She scrambled to the kitchen, grabbed a knife and ran into the backyard. A shadow stood over the donkey. Benito continued screaming in between the sounds of a giant rock smashing into the muscles of his belly. Magdalena thought only a demon could be standing in front of her.

It was Alonzo. Alonzo kept beating the donkey with full force until it stopped breathing. Magdalena sobbed silently and ran toward Alonzo with the knife. She stabbed him in the shoulder. He shoved her down. With the knife still in her hand she grabbed the back of his leg and took the blade to his Achilles tendon. It separated with a sound like a gunshot. Alonzo screamed and held the back of his leg as blood trickled through the cracks of his fingers. He looked back at Magdalena and spit toward her as he picked himself back up.

Alonzo limped toward the house. Magdalena's heart dropped when she saw flames illuminating the house. She searched for the source of the fire. Alonzo found Magdalena's library. She hid her books underneath the linen closet. Her maps and journals burned inside her hidden library. He was going to burn her and the babies inside her house. The house she painted bright blue. The house with the garden of herbs she planted together with her girl and boy. Alonzo wanted to own her. Magdalena pleaded at Alonzo to stop. She sobbed as she heard her little girl and boy start to scream.

Alonzo doused himself in gasoline in front of the children. He smiled at Magdalena and flames filled the room. Alonzo fell to the ground and his body spasmed. He laughed as his body started bubbling from the flames. Magdalena ran toward the children. She grabbed them both and tried to run out of the room. Smoke filled her lungs and her last memories. The last thing she remembered was holding onto both of her babies as they burned alive because of the cruel man she once loved.

The boy taps Diana on the shoulder and tells her to turn right. They are on the haunted bridge. According to Frida, a woman with a demon's face lives underneath. She jumps on top of your car and crunches the metal to tell you to keep out. Diana stops the car on the bridge. This is the haunted space Frida wanted to explore. Fog surrounds them. It seeps into the car and the taste of the cloud sits on Diana's tongue.

The radio comes on. It sounds like a whisper and then a soft cry. The crying stops. Heavy breathing and gurgled moaning goes in and out of the radio. Frida tells Diana she's afraid. Diana looks over at Frida and tells her to cover her ears. Screams come through the radio speakers. Diana tries to turn off the radio but the screaming continues. The woman on the radio sounds like she is in mourning. She screams and then she takes in a deep breath and she wails in a deep voice. The screaming stops. The fog disappears.

The headlights of the car point at a woman in a white dress with a purple scarf around her head. Smoke is coming off her skin. She moves slowly and she limps as she stumbles toward the car. Her left foot is partially intact. Pieces of it scrape off as she approaches the car. Her right foot is a rounded nub. She gets on her hands and knees and begins to drag herself toward the car. Diana looks over to the passenger seat. Frida is gone.

Diana covers her mouth and screams into her palms. She looks in the back seat and the boy and girl are gone too. Loud slow thumps start on the roof of the car. Diana is shaking and frantically opens the car door. She falls out and onto the ground and sees the woman in the scarf standing on top of the car. The woman shrieks and then hisses. The woman points at the water. Diana picks herself up and lunges into the water.

She swims under the bridge. Under the arch, she slams her fists against the concrete. She tears at the brick with her nails. She knows the creature has escaped inside these walls because the little boy told her so. She shoves her shoulder into the brick. One of the blocks budges. Diana kicks the loose brick in. She digs into the freed space until the hole is big enough for her to fit into. She clutches at loose roots and swims to the other side. She's in a tunnel big enough for a car to fit through. Candles flicker atop sconces. She looks up and animal skulls line the ceiling. Diana swims toward the entrance of the tunnel and picks herself up onto a ledge. Pink ribbon floats and twirls in the water. Diana screams as loud as she can until her throat burns. She sprints through the skull tunnel looking for Frida.

Her body slams into something and then she feels a hard kick to her gut. A donkey. She holds onto her side and gasps for air. Diana looks around and she is surrounded by donkeys. She claws at the ground and picks herself up. She walks slowly around the animals. They all wear jewelry made of beads around their necks and some of them have gems and stones on the crowns of their heads and down their faces. As she stumbles further into the tunnel, all of them turn to face her and step forward in synchronization. Rushing water erupts inside the tunnel and knocks Diana off of her feet. Diana's eyes fill with white light.

Diana is spit out of the tunnel. Covered in mud, she looks up and sees Frida holding a flashlight in her mouth and digging into the earth. Diana sprints to Frida and picks her up into her arm and kisses her forehead. Frida cries and tells Diana she has to find a donkey named Benito. He's under the ground and they need to make an altar to him and the donkey woman. Diana doesn't question Frida's request. She begins to dig as fast as she can. The sun announces itself in the horizon. Diana and Frida keep digging. Several hours into digging, the earth gives them what they are looking for. The skull of a donkey and then its spine, and several pieces of a rib cage. Diana and Frida pick up the pieces and place them under overgrowing nopales reaching for the sun. Frida picks flowers and leaves and offers them to the altar. Diana finds smooth stones to stack on top of one another as a marker for Benito's final burial site. Frida holds the photo of her mom with the pregnant belly and she kisses it before she places the photograph next to Benito's skull. She writes into her notebook: say hi to my mom. She's the moon. You can call her Luna.

Magdalena is surrounded by white light. Gabino is born and she holds onto him tight. She kisses the birthmark on his tiny shoulder. She nuzzles him and breathes in his full head of hair. Elena is born and Magdalena holds her in her other arm. She kisses Elena on the forehead. The light pierces through her line of vision and Magdalena sees herself as a child. She's picking sunflower seeds and gathering them in a giant red bowl. The bowl is so big, she naps in it sometimes. She chews on some of the sunflower seeds and she spits their shells at the sky. She sits in the kitchen, next to her mother's parakeets and sings about the sunshine. She is surrounded by white light. She breathes for a matter of seconds and then it all stops. It all stops and she is now light and silence.

US

Amelia Gray

"Some say that evil has existed there for centuries. Others feel that it emanated from the road that ran through that portion of the valley. It apparently was so strong that even the trees were stunted by it. But regardless of the source of whatever wrongs have occurred there over the years, locals say that the Cult House is not a place you want to stay in – or even around – for very long, whether it's day or night."

- Patricia A. Martinelli, *Haunted Delaware*

Devil would have at our time of greatest suffering when the town pushed us out and killed the ground behind us and burned it past the fulcrum point and no sooner was when we found the House. From the flames we ran and ran we slowed to a trot. Slowed to a walk and wander. For days we wandered through the woods and lo. The House. On the land at center.

We five all the same. Name and face all the same. Five boys named Tad. Our hair red our face thick pale and jowl. We stood no dog found one and cut her to five. Best to share we learned. We are legion. We did squirrel and yard bird lay their bones to fester. We kept fat and happy. Devil would have we were alone. A bird came to cross the dale we would quick curse it to drop in our pot. To find our psychic net. We kept a nice fire of trash and tires. Would that the bird knew.

To make our spelling star round the House we never touched Its walls or locked Its window pane or steps or brick for It was sacred. We slept on boards one eye among us watching the House yellow-gold and whole. We fresh in our power and draped in it. We servile beast. We strong and sure. We listen to the earth to its sound to the south. Being what you don't know will kill you.

To say they did come and brought their trucks and tents and cans of beer. Boys and little girls as from school. We did articulate our joy with howls and moaning. They come to discover! Their campsite circle the bending trees the girls their lips the sweet girls cudding to their boys. They make a fire to settle in they open cans of beer and food they watch and wait they far from home.

Their elders lived to cross us and made it law to never try. NEVER TRY THE LEGION
TAD they said. We saw them in our sleep. They knew but not their kids they knew how
we were and came to be. The town a mass of good and humble folk the county line
a fulcrum the trees and House a weight to keep the balance the five of us crucial. As
they say Good needs Tad. But now these boys and little girls have willed off the weight
these little boys and baby girls.

We all of us wait the House thrums a beating heart. It makes to speak we draw near
it makes to tell us. We draw near. TOUCH ME it growls we press palms to it TOUCH
EACH OTHER we clasp one arm around the other and press the House it makes a
Dark Circuit there a razor sense all of them those boys and girls we see to make them
TOUCH THEM the House screams ear to ear inside our baby boy brain cross the circuit five. Touch fire to sense we land on our backs laid out like cord wood drymouthed
cordwood our hands palms jagged broken glass unbleeding our hands palms weapons
against. A gift from the House! We holler and clap and shards sprinkle snowfire.

Run through the woods we screeching to them we to see these guests to TOUCH THEM
we good students we boys like the rest we make to know them we hear their noises we
smell their good food we see their campfire we hear their singing WE see their bodies
WE see their faces WE see their faces WE see their faces THEY DO NOT SEE US

Hierarchy of Meats

Justin Hudnall

"Missouri's main monster is clearly Momo, the Missouri monster. Momo takes on many shapes and forms, but typically remains something close to a bipedal humanoid that lacks social interaction skills, is impossibly sneaky, and clearly has personal hygiene issues – sort of like a neighbor, but not around as much."

- James Strait, Mark Moran & Mark Scuerman, *Weird Missouri*

A thing is always, and only, just meat in the end.

These hang-down bits I yanked from the dog's throat are now meat, meat that has transferred from the canine's ownership to my own.

My arm, where the dog's teeth have punctured and torn and raked the skin in protest, that's just a thing of meat, but still mine.

The woman and baby the dog will nourish, they're meat too, but meat I have made arrangements with.

See we have names and titles for one another, which are falsehoods, but polite courtesy is important to keep within a home.

But to think I nearly killed myself for feeling I'd disappointed that courtesy, now that's disturbing.

Momo is going to show you what's real though.

I was so scared—SO SCARED—before I swallowed his lesson.

Just hours prior I was huddling in the woods, staring into a bird's nest of broken glass and plastic and mud that had been my only pair of glasses.

And I'd decided it was a message: a message telling me the best thing I could possibly do with my life would be to end it, and without delay, by jamming the barrel of my rifle under my chin and launching my skull and what little brains it contained out the top of my dumbshit head.

I'd thought about suicide plenty in my twenty-five years, often for the comfort it brought me when I couldn't sleep over the sounds of my wife and son breathing up all the air in the cottage we share.

Out here in the woods alone though, I could imagine my death in a vacuum, and that made me the closest thing to happy I'd been since I couldn't remember.

I'd finally be free of "potential," and all the women who'd accused me of having it, from Mother to Wife to Wife's Mother.

Sometimes when I could stand to hear no more about the stuff of potential, I'd challenge them to give me a name or direction for how they saw I might act upon it, but something urgent in another room always caused them to drift away before revealing their vision for my redemption, and I'd go back to the Xbox.

Here in the woods of Pike County, Missouri though, my corpse could be the final word on what all that potential would ever lead to.

Our hand-out check hadn't come in before the three-day holiday, and the pantry was empty except for a handful of jerky, and some cheese sticks that didn't need to go in the refrigerator.

The baby's crying made it impossible to ignore the failure of myself, and Janelle's silence drowned out what little common sense I had.

So I wadded up the meat and cheese into a mashed cylinder of cling wrap, stuck them into my jacket pocket, and set out to be a hero, meaning to bag us some game so we could have a dinner with the special dignity only enjoyed when I hadn't had to beg Janelle's mother to pay for it.

That was a mistake, because hero was never in my character, which was actually entirely that of a fat, dumb, useless idiot who never graduated high school even though he could have, who wasn't even all that good at videogames for all his playing them, who never had the grit to sell crystal like his cousins, who told everyone he was too good for the blue vest of Walmart but couldn't get a job from anyone else to prove it.

Just a bulging toolshed of flesh, with legs the size and shape of a carcass hanging from a hook in a slaughterhouse, and whose trunk was so long his shadow looked like a massive Twinkie.

That was all I knew of myself before Momo taught me the way of things.

Not the knock-off bigfoot who never brought in a tourist since he was first hallucinated by some other poor man, whose wife and daughter thought to get rich before having him treated for his ailment, not the lie.

I used to hate those women, but it tickles me now that I know Momo was real all along, just not the way that serves their kind.

The path that led me to him, that began at my front door and took me into the woods across the road, was only meant to last a short outing, but I lost track of time, enjoying the quiet of being alone in the woods until the hours grew lightless, and my food eaten, and I realized I'd ran out of time, and never once saw a single squirrel the whole while.

The little shits who'd never let a picnic at the lake pass in peace were less than ghosts now that I needed them.

I'd marched through hollers and gullies, abandoning one path for another as the mood struck me, never accepting the meatlessness of the land until the light faltered.

Then I slipped on a patch of loose rocks and plowed my face, with my only glasses attached, straight into a wash.

And that, I decided, was enough to go and die over, before anybody could ask my mother-in-law for money in my presence again.

Life and all its many jagged corners could sit a permanent time-out in the fuck-it bucket, I was done.

If I came home empty-handed, the door would open unto Janelle's hungry eyes, and I would have to say to them, "There were no squirrels out."

And I could not bring myself to say those words because I could not understand them myself.

It sounded like a lie even after having just lived it.

So I sat in my pool of broken glass in the dark, working up the nerve to add a final and fist-sized pock to my head, and to force Janelle to go save herself.

I had the gun loaded and the safety off and the barrel under my chin and my toe out of its shoe to stamp the trigger, and was happy to do what would have come next except I heard myself thinking *this would be the perfect way to go if only that fucking dog would stop barking.*

Then I had to stop and think about what I'd just thought.

A dog barking meant a backyard, and for it to go un-hushed for so long meant no one was home.

Stealing from a stranger's kitchen under the circumstances seemed to have an almost nobility about it.

Every decision not to commit suicide in my lifetime has been followed by a doubling down on the very path that led me to it, and this time was no different.

So off I went, blurry-eyed, towards the barking.

It didn't take but a few minutes before I broke through the bramble upon a dark little shack the woods had grown in on since being built.

A bumperless Chevy Tahoe, once blue but now equal parts orange rust, sat on a plot of land at the end of a path, one I could see led back out to a main road.

That was the way of these woods and why I'd stayed out of them for so long.

They created a geography of the mind, where a man could be as lost and far from help as any man ever was, and still be ten minutes by car from getting himself more jerky at Gas Mart.

The truck belonged to Marcus Bridges, a regular at the bowling alley bar Janelle's mother tended.

I knew it by the bumper sticker on the back window that read, "if you're going to ride my ass at least pull my hair."

Mr. Bridges was famous for his moments of paranoia, so I kept as low as my size allowed while feeling my way across the chicken-wire fence running the length of his property.

Then I thought to check my watch, and saw it was long past seven.

It being Friday, chances were in my favor Marcus would already be at least an hour into a dead drunk that would carry him well into Saturday afternoon before he'd reappear, shaking and pained, to get himself right again wherever Black Velvet was sold.

Until then, anyone could walk right up to his door, kick it in, and make themselves dinner from his cupboard without worrying about waking the sad sack of donut batter and pain, propped up by skeleton alone.

So I steadied my bulk against a post to heave one of my ham hocks over, but couldn't quite, and instead tore the whole section down.

The dog I'd heard barking back when my gun was in my mouth stood like a coffee table, tied around the neck by a rope to a tree grown wild next to Marcus's shack, a brown mutt only a little bigger than an old-timey doctor's bag, full of noise but without the muscle to mean it.

If Marcus got his animal as protection he'd be right to feel disappointed, because the little fucker only barked marginally more at a gun-toting giant walking up on his land as he'd done at the nothing that came before me.

Up on the porch lay a scattering of things a healthier man might have kept indoors, things like pots and pans and eating utensils and glassware, some shattered, some whole.

Mildewed titty mags, the kind I'd have been thrilled to find as a boy, were stacked into a knee-high tower beside the front door, turned to soggy pulp from the wet air.

I gave the door an obligatory tap tap tap with the barrel of the rifle before I swung it inwards a crack, after no response came.

A single ceiling bulb without cover flicked on when I found the switch, yellowed from smoke.

Nothing stirred inside, at least not that I could hear over the bark fucking never ending barking of the dog, and so I invited myself in.

Half expecting, maybe hoping, to see my first dead body, I instead found the reason why so much of old Marcus's stuff was sitting out on the porch.

Rats or coons or other sharp-toothed creatures had fashioned an entrance into his shack by tunneling through the eaves near where his potbelly stove pipe joined to the ceiling, and which Marcus had either ignored or been too drunk to notice until the last rain storm passed through—and it had been a doozy—pissing grey water all over his VHS collection that mostly consisted of dogs playing one form of human sport or another.

Despite the weather damage and gross-old-man state of affairs, there was still plenty to suggest he hadn't abandoned his home: boxes of mac n' cheese in animal shapes were stacked throughout a particle board bookcase along with cans of soup, the treasure I'd planned to raid.

There was no alcohol around but that was to be expected, but I craved it if only to slow my heart that had been beating to the breaking point for far longer than I noticed, but I noticed it then.

Especially then, when I was reading the story of Marcus Bridge's life writ in filth across his home, each corner a chapter, like the remnants of a flannel shirt he'd left on the floor, now made as much of the stuff its owner had wiped off as the original fabric.

Peanut butter, semen, blood, engine oil, tobacco juice, cotton, plastic buttons, phlegm.

His unmade bed was no worse off than the bed of any other single man I knew, and all told in fairness the scene might just be a sad old fart's house for sure, but not a crime scene.

Unless writing on your own floor with roof tar was a crime, which I'm sure it isn't.

It halted me though to see it, would have given me a scare to read any word written large in black, corpulent letters across linoleum, but Marcus had picked a great one for a reader who'd been through such an ordeal as I had, alone, at night, and unexpected.

"TRUTH," he'd writ, just like that. In roof tar. On his floor.

And I swear the worst part wasn't even the fact that he'd taken a solid shit next to it, which he had, like a statement on what he thought about living indoors.

The worst part was the little chair, the only piece of furniture in the room besides the bed, that he'd arranged above his "truth," and on that chair he'd placed a book, and on the book, a plastic old person pill organizer.

Like he'd known another was coming, like he'd hoped it would be found, making me feel like an animal, sensing too late it was trapped, after the fact.

A thinking beast seen by another as meat.

The book looked like one of the relics we had in the community library, without a paper cover, bound in dull yellow canvas from a grandfatherly era.

No title was printed across its spine, and the pages had been soaked by some wetness for long so as to leave them impossible to separate.

Like old Marcus had left it out just to brag he'd been the last man to read and learn from it whatever he had, and even with my heart throbbing so it scared me I was mad at him for it.

But the pill case that sat upon the book was still six out of seven days full.

Only Saturday was empty, the others contained measured portions of yellow-brown flakes, somewhere between rusted paint chips, maybe crystals, maybe dried leaves, impossible to tell.

I wetted a finger and used it to spoon up a serving to my nose, which caught hints of blood and sick and wrong sweetness, like stuff meant to stay inside a living thing and not outside.

The smell made me think about an ex-tweaker pastor I'd been made to spend a summer with while a teenager.

For all his love of Christ and the sobriety, Pastor couldn't stop himself from talking about meth like a lost love, far more compelling than he ever talked about Jesus.

But one thing he said stuck with me: he said, "An addict doesn't do drugs or drink to get high or low, he uses because he just wants to feel different than how he does."

And at that moment, because I was sorely not happy wherever the fuck I was at, I took the advice he hadn't meant to give and licked the flakes down my throat.

I waited, tuned into every signal my body was sending, looked past symptoms and pangs and palpitations I'd ignored for years, and waited and waited until the only new thing I felt was hunger.

A hunger that felt without bottom and that I despaired at the thought of ever satisfying.

A hunger that clamped my jaw down and ground my teeth till little bits of bone swam in my spit, and I swallowed them too.

But then the dog's bark bark bark fucking barking brought me back to the moment and I clutched the gun I hadn't the eyesight to shoot straight anymore, and to no one's greater surprise than my own, turned back around and walked out the door to survey the dark beyond it.

The dog on its chain, stretched out like the stem of an arrow, was yelling and shouting in its weak language against the presence of a thing in the trees.

It came to me then that the dog was not barking at me, never had been.

And of course no squirrels had been out.

There was something else in the woods to be scared of, and I was then.

A fleeting thought sparked: that maybe whatever was out there, I might kill it first, and bring it back home, and be some kind of a hero still.

Justify Janelle's stupid love into a thing to be deserved, and wanted.

Beat down what was so big and scary that the mother-in-law would get to thinking she could be next if she didn't start being nicer.

Maybe she would be. Nicer. Next.

Or maybe the thing would kill me instead, and that would be just as good.

I prayed to the childhood monster that didn't exist, to Momo: come and tear my throat out before my cowardice sends me running to the road, and a passing driver's compassion, where my weakness would make a fucking news story out of me for all to laugh at and remember for the rest of my days.

Just let something not be my fault.

Instead I called out Marcus's name, a statement, not a question.

Marcus.

Where are you Marcus.

I called out that I was the man whose name had been Dan Windmiller.

It sounded like a lie and so I only said it the once.

I walked to the edge of the clearing, to where the dark became all branches and fear, and I stared into it for minutes, hours; the dark doesn't count time, it's all one until the ugly blue of dawn ends it.

I stood and stared into it until my back teeth became dust, until my belly rumbled with cravings I couldn't understand, until my cock became hard and full, until I saw the thing's eyes staring back at me, yellow, like the book inside the shack, like the flakes I'd ate in fear.

The eyes of Momo, nothing like the lie told for the hope of tourists' crumpled dollars that never did come from his invention to this poor as shit town of Nothingfuck, Missouri.

"Do you see it?" cried Marcus Bridges from somewhere farther out in the dark than I could see, only beginning down the path he'd cut for decades. "It sees you! It knows what you need!"

And I knew then too what I needed.

I knew I had never been lost in the woods, but rather lost my whole life.

Knew that Momo was no monster at all but a tradition, carried on by fatherless generations, ever since the first poor man knew God was no better than a carnie who rigged his games against the townies.

Since the first poor man decided to turn his back forever on all the prizes he'd never had a chance of winning anyhow, who'd learned the truth by staring into those same yellowed eyes I stared into then, understanding at last the pain had already been drunk too long and too deep to fear it any more.

He laughed loud then like a great victory had come upon him, and so did I, though soft enough to still find him out in the dark by his noise, and grip my hands up around his scratchy loose cheeks.

His fist pulped my right eye some as a greeting, but still he laughed all the while and so did I, even as I drove his weak old skull against the tree's strong trunks that stood all about us. Marcus collapsed against the strength of one who'd carry on what he was ready to let go of.

I set him up nice against one of those same tree's base, arranged him like a man sleeping in a shady place, where no judgment could burn him further, then kissed the wet slap of his forehead and turned back towards his shack knowing what his final wish would be.

The dog backed away from me then, back to the edge of its chain, digging its hind legs in against the hard ground and trying to jerk its anchor out.

The doomed creatures of the earth always look so funny when they're about to meet their end don't they just.

It made me laugh some but I knew there was work to be done, so I caught the sweet little mongrel up by the neck with my left hand and worked the great round fingers of my right into the soft part of its cheek to start, then back behind its boneless molars, where it couldn't get the leverage to bite, and forced more and more of my hand inside the widening and convulsing opening I created, working the lower jaw down farther from the upper until at last with a little elbow grease and a heave it gave way with a crack, and the lesser unfortunate's eye's rolled up and I punched down into the spider web of pulp I found there, wrest the trophy free, and threw them upon the ground.

Then it was the dog's turn to be silent and the man who howled.

It was a sign of what powers I'd been given that I could run without sight straight from the spot, with the dog's meat across my neck, keeping the main road to my right as I stayed in the dark.

Just before the Gas Mart I sprinted across the road and stayed to the drainage ditch where I could barrel full-tilt past the land of a dozen properties before arriving at the lot claimed by the meat I call family.

I kicked at our door, again and again, feeling the lights come on and the confused mutterings of Janelle and the boy rise in pitch as they scrambled to throw it open and greet me, and the feast I brought them.

Now here is where I invite you to join us in our brand new morning: scream with them, as they scream and scream and scream with joy at the new day I have brought us all, free and honest creatures at last.

MARIE
ENGER
2016

Son of Goatman

Andrea Kneeland

"Prince George's County's infamous Goatman has been described as a white-colored, half-human, half-animal creature with goat hooves, a narrow face, and circular horns. Sometimes the monster runs on all fours, other times it races upright. It's also been said to resemble drawings of the ancient Greek god Pan, playing a flute. But its more often been spotted wielding a deadly ax.'"

- Ed Okonowicz, *Monsters of Maryland*

If you've seen any of my movies, you might think that you know something about me. Or maybe you think that I'm lucky, that I did it because I wanted to. But the simple truth is that it's really hard to find a job when you're half-goat. You think anyone wants to hire a dude with this abomination for a body? Nasty, matted-up fur on the bottom half, cloven hooves, a penis that no normal human woman would want anything to do with.

Ever since I got back from the San Fernando Valley, I've been living in a trailer about a mile off from Cry Baby Bridge. It's the same trailer I lived in out in California, but this spot here is a lot more secluded. I can't decide if I like it or not. I can't decide if I like being back home in Hyattsville or not.

I did find a new job out here, and I liked that, for a while, and was feeling pretty good about being home. I still couldn't get away from the porn—the only place that wanted to hire me was the sex store a couple towns over, that shitty run-down pit that smelled like ball sweat and mouse turds, the one that shook every time the train went by and that didn't have any bathroom or running water so every time I had to take a piss I had to do it out back near the dumpsters, like an animal. But still, as crappy as it was working there, I had reached a point in my life where I would rather sell porn than to star in it.

It's one thing, I guess, to be in porn because you're really good at it, or because you like it, or because you're good-looking. It's another thing when someone wants to film you because you're a freak.

Anyway, it felt pretty good to be home and pretty good to have an almost-normal job and having an almost-normal job made me feel almost-normal. A little less lonely. But then I found out that the reason they hired me wasn't in spite of who I was—it was *because of* who I was. Thought it would bring in customers. They threw a huge fan event, "Goatman in Person," $20 cover for a meet-and-greet. I didn't know anything about it until I showed up that night and my boss, Bruce, opened up the door and greeted me with a big shit-eating grin.

The point is that I quit right then and there. Feeling pretty low about it now. I'd call up Bruce and ask for my old job back, but I was so mad that I spit on his ugly bald head before I left. So now I'm back where I started.

Not quite where I started. The Valley was better than this. I'm not saying that I never arrived on a set and thought things looked bad, not saying that I never had to fuck a girl who, minutes before, had been cowering in the corner, tears welling up in her eyes, shaking with repulsion until someone found the right drugs to calm her down. Especially in the early days of my career, there was a lot of that.

But, look, I never wanted to hurt anyone.

I didn't have a mother. I'm not trying to make you feel sorry for me, telling you that. It's just that to tell you about myself, I have to tell you about my dad, and when you tell people about your dad, they always follow up asking about your mom, so I want to cut it off before it starts. I don't know who she was and, unless my dad spent his whole life lying to me, he didn't know who she was either. Work that out however you want.

My father was a lonely man. I take after him, so I understand why he was lonely, and why he'd want a son just like him, but I still can't really forgive him for it. He knew better than anyone what it was like to be a monster.

People used to get us mixed up, before he died. Didn't realize that there were two Goatmen living in Maryland. Didn't have room enough in their brain to believe that we could be two different people, that even though one of us might like to sneak up on teenagers at night waving an axe and shrieking like an ape, the other one might just be a normal guy. Or want to be a normal guy. Maybe it was harder for my dad, who lived his first twenty years as a normal person, just a mind-your-own business janitor at a USDA research lab before one of the scientists offered him an extra $100 to run a few "harmless" experiments. I guess I can understand where the pent-up rage came from.

But that axe-murderer, he's not me. And no one wants to believe that.

Now, there are three suited men in low-pulled baseball caps sitting in lawn chairs pulled into a tight semi-circle outside my trailer. One of them is smoking a cigar. The end of the cigar turns a nearly neon orange as he sucks in, tiny flecks of fire floating away against the darkness. These three men, they don't believe that I'm not a murderer, either.

When they called me about making this movie, I misunderstood. I mean, I got that they wanted me to wave an axe around, that they wanted to make some stupid porno based on The Goatman legend. It's not like I haven't done those kinds of movies before.

What I didn't understand was that they wanted it for real. That they were talking about snuff. I should have understood that, when they told me how much they'd pay me. But I'd been dumpster diving for weeks when they called, and all I thought about was how good a steak would taste; not why, who, how?

"Look, man," I'm saying to the one on the left, in the brown suit, the one with a face like Goebbels who seems to be the brains of the operation. "Look, we can't film it here. This is where I *live*, man. What about the blood? How am I—"

He flaps his bony wrist at me, swatting an invisible fly. "We'll get you a new trailer," he says, as he squints up at the blackening horizon. "Authenticity is important."

Then he turns and walks away, pops the trunk of one of the towncars they drove in with, and begins to unpack lighting equipment. Cigar is still puffing in slow, smooth drags, and the man to his right, as if he could tell what I was thinking, has pulled out a revolver and rested it casually on his knee. It occurs to me for the first time that I might die tonight. That maybe the snuff doesn't end with the girl I haven't seen yet. My palms start to sweat.

I point at the gun. "I can't perform if you're gonna aim that thing at me." Revolver doesn't move or acknowledge that I've said a word. "Hey!" I yell, this time, over at Goebbels, who has now opened the trunk of the second Lincoln. He doesn't look up. "Get your buddy here to put his gun away."

Goebbels doesn't answer, busy as he is with carrying a struggling woman to the front steps of my trailer. As he passes me, I get a glimpse of her face, terrified eyes shiny and wide like puddles of kerosene. Her screams are muffled by duct tape, her whole body spasming like her insides are made out of electricity. I don't have time to turn away or even bend over before I vomit. At this, Cigar lets out a guffaw and then a disappointed sigh. "I wish the camera had been running for that." Then, like a cartoon with a light bulb appearing above its head, his eyes go wide. He pulls out his phone and points it at me. "Pre-production outtakes!" he shouts, giggling.

I walk to the trunk Goebbels had retrieved the woman from, partly to have an excuse to get away from Cigar's camera, partly from dread-laced curiosity: what if the trunk was packed with more people that they wanted me to kill, pressed flesh to flesh like oily, dead-eyed sardines? But all I find is a coil of rope and an axe.

I crouch for a minute to dry heave, then I pick up the axe and return to the trailer, my head airy and buzzing. Lights that I know aren't there are flashing against my eyes in shattering bursts. My rib bones feel like they're hell-bent on crushing my lungs. Cigar is still sitting in the same spot, recording, but Goebbels and Revolver have turned their backs to me, preoccupied with the girl.

I split Revolver's head open first. The movement is so natural to me that I wonder for a moment if there is some genetic basis for the way it feels while I'm swinging the axe, so magical and right and true, my rib bones opening back up and the air flooding into my lungs in big, healthy bursts.

I have never felt so alive.

Revolver slumps to the ground, curly ribbons of tightly coiled pink meat blossoming out from the opening I've made in his skull. A brain is really a gorgeous thing when you see it up close. Viscerally stunning.

The axe flies backward and down again—it seems that it's moving of its own accord, not interested in leaving me time to ponder the wonders of beauty of the human body—and sinks deep into the dead man's back, straight through, the blade driving clean through his body and into the earth beneath.

Goebbels has, obviously, begun to run, but the idiot is so terrified that he is stumbling, falling down over and over again, nowhere near either of the towncars. I will overtake him easily. I notice Cigar from the corner of my eye, an even bigger idiot, stunned like a pig about to be slaughtered, still sitting in the lawn chair, phone still held aloft. I grin for his camera.

I do something a little different with Goebbels and swing toward one of his flailing hands. The hand splits clean off and flies upward in graceful arc, like a featherless bird plummeting through the twilight sky. Poetic.

Next, I hack off a foot. He falls sharply to the ground and I kick him in the head with a hoof, then bend down to turn him over to his back. I want to see what his heart looks like. My blade sinks into the jelly of his stomach and as I pull back out to realign and aim for the chest, I hear a sharp explosion behind me, like a cherry bomb.

The speed with which the girl managed to get free was either a testament to her prow-ess or a sign that whoever tied her up in the first place was really terrible at his job. Either way, she's standing over the fat man's corpse with a gun.

I'm grinning so hard I feel like my face might fall off and I trot toward her. I'm imme-diately filled with a deep affection for her, my partner in crime, and there is something so familiar about her that I widen my arms as I approach, as if she's family. She lets me get about three feet away before she turns the gun on me.

I stop mid-trot, arms still spread wide, holding the axe aloft. And at that moment, I realize that she is family. Sort of. I can't remember her name, but she's been with me for half a decade, a shadowy spirit that follows me everywhere.

She was the co-star in my first video, the one with titles like HORNY MAN-GOAT PISS FUCK WHORE. The one that went sort of underground viral, at least viral enough to get a subreddit dedicated to me, to get me my own AMA and, in turn, more movie of-fers, a higher going rate. She was one of the girls who couldn't be calmed down by any of the drugs the crew had on hand.

I struggle to remember her name. She's screaming at me "Fuck you, you freak piece of shit," things like that. I stop hearing her. Her voice is background noise. I am laser-focused.

I push off the ground with my haunches like the earth is a goddamned trampoline and two seconds later, she's missing an arm and the gun is at her feet. I watch the blood snake out from the severed arm in little gory rivers, the blood more black then red beneath the moonlight, until the gun is sitting in a lake of it. She is still standing in the same spot, screaming and screaming and screaming.

I do feel sorry for her, even though she was going to kill me. But even more than I feel sorry, I feel the adrenaline coursing up through my veins, my lungs opening wide to breathe in the trees and the sky and the stars and the planets and the heavens and everything pure in this universe and I feel *good*, good like I've never felt before in my life, not before tonight.

I swing again.

Scape Ore Scramble

Jennifer D. Corley

"Long-time residents of the area reminded others that Carolinian Native American tribes had an extensive mythology about the Inzignanin, a race of amphibious humanoid creatures that had once lived in the swamps and rivers of the Carolinas. Who was to say that all such creatures had died out?"

- Brad Steiger, *Real Monsters, Gruesome Critters, and Beasts from the Darkside*

There was a time when I scrambled up rocks, after I had scooted down them, chasin after a wheel nut, then decidin it wasn't that important after I felt like I could be goin down for miles and miles and never come back. I knew that wasn't the case, it just felt like that. And when I turned around, the top of the road seemed so far away, the beam of my headlights seemed to be cuttin through the fog, yet so dimly, so far away from me, but that couldn't be right, *was it so far away?* I shouldn't have smoked with Rudy before I left, I should've saved it for home, but I liked hangin out with Rudy and shootin the shit with him, so I did it, I got so frazzled at work sometimes, so I did it, and I didn't think it was that big a deal, but fuckin dammit, it felt so far down the hill now, and I couldn't see anything, except maybe somethin shining way far down there even further, and who's to say if that's even the nut? I didn't want to go trying to find out. I could go *down there*, or I could turn around and go *up there*. So I turned around and went up there, back up, and it actually felt easier goin up, because I had a definite goal in sight, I wanted to get to them headlights so bad, rather than just runnin like a baby, wobblin down into the dark nothingness hopin to see more glint in the black. I was wedgin my feet and my hands nimble-like, in between rocks, I was gettin up there fast, the kudzu vine was grabbin at my feet but it was actually kinda helping me, like carpet, giving me somethin to walk up, footholds, rather than just slick swamp rock.

When I climbed over the guardrail, I was relieved. Never so happy to cut my hand on jagged metal, where somebody before me had made a mistake at that spot. I looked at the rail. It was red, but not from my blood. It was red car paint, old.

I sat, up against the rail, catchin my breath, lookin at the tire missin a nut. It pissed me off; I took pride in my car. But oh well, I could get another nut. I just liked the ones I had and didn't wanna be a little bitch and not try to get the one that rolled off the road.

But that was before. That was before when I scrambled on rocks; I don't do that no more, I don't play at bullshit, I don't stop on the side of the road at night for no shaky tires, I don't rest on roadsides. I don't take pride in my car. I had to get rid of Ol' Lucy—I sold her to Rudy for 300 dollars when I finally couldn't take it anymore, couldn't take gettin into her, couldn't take the reminders, couldn't bear seein the bite marks, the scratches, the rust marks where I never bothered to fix her. Couldn't stand bein reminded that I was a fuckin joke. People laughed when I sobbed, sittin in that fuckin car at night, after night, after night, and when I drove past the spot with the red on the rail, where the blood had dripped from my hand onto the asphalt where the glint from the swamp might have been a nut, or it might have been an eye, it might have been one of those fuckin eyes lookin at me and I didn't even know it, I just knew that I had to go back up to my car. And people made a fuckin joke out of it, out of me, and walked around in fuckin costumes and said Lizard Man wants you to eat their fried okra at their restaurant or Lizard Man wants you to buy their T-Shirt or Lizard Man wants you to buy some property by the creek *or how about this: Lizard Man wants to rip your fuckin eyeballs out, nobody says that one, do they, nobody says Lizard Man wants to tear the roof off your car while you sit in it and shit inside your pants like a fuckin baby when you're a grown-ass man, while you cry and beg for God to save you and say you'll never treat Lindsey bad again, and you'll never smoke weed again, and you're sorry you ain't done more with the life Mama gave you and you're just sorry, you're just sorry sorry sorry, and you can't find nothin inside your car to fight back with, and what the fuck you gonna fight back with anyway? This nigga is tryin to tear the roof off your car. He's pullin and pullin and breakin windows and all you can concentrate on is the mouth that's open so wide, so pink, so full of sharp shark teeth, and long claws, scrapin at the paint and the metal, beautiful Ol' Lucy gettin pulled at like he wants to shred barbecue it feels like, and the only thing that makes him stop is the lion's roar of a huge F-150 on boggers comin round the corner. You ain't never been so glad for a redneck truck in all your life. That thing waddled off like a man in scuba flippers, but fast, over the rail and down into the darkness, where you had just been, except he went further, deeper, beyond. And the men in the F-150 didn't see nothin, and they just drove right on by, 'cause all they saw was a black dude sittin in a beat-to-shit car on the side of the road. Is that fuckin funny? Can you make a bumper sticker for that?*

And that was the last time I scrambled up rocks.

Two of them in my family wore gold necklaces. One necklace featured a goddamn huge dollar sign; the other showcased the cursive name "Fuchsia." It wasn't really her name, she just liked the color and wanted people to call her that. It worked; people assumed it was her name when they saw the word danglin around her neck. Fuckin men around here would read her chest, a slow smile spreadin over their faces, tellin her *what a pretty name* it was; and whenever she thanked them, I knew they wondered what color her insides were.

She was my little sister. She had heard the story before, she grew up with it, but she tried to distance herself from it. She didn't want to be known as the sister of That Guy Who Saw The Lizard Man. She just wanted to be Fuchsia.

Uncle Chris—my mama's brother—was the one with the big love of money. He flashed that dollar sign necklace like it was a real thousand dollar bill hangin from his neck. He told Fuchsia the story behind the swamp's name—Scape Ore—when she was little, and she always disliked him for it. She thought it was crazy for a man to tell the story to any little girl, much less his own niece. But he told the story with so much dramatic flair, she wasn't sure if it was true or if he made it up. She never liked the swamp because of it, felt like she was cursed, like maybe all women were cursed. Uncle Chris told her about how people called it Scape Ore Swamp their whole lives not knowin that it was short for Escaped Whore Swamp, named after a hooker that got chased out of town in the 1700s. The people were gonna kill her but she ran off into the swamp and lost them. Chris always acted out the story like he was the hooker in the muck, almost dancin like he was wadin into muddy swamp water, pretendin like he was hikin layers of old skirt up around his hips, laughin and laughin, gesturing like he was wavin hair out of his eyes and over his shoulder while he squealed in lady-disgust over gettin wet in the dark swamp water. Fuchsia didn't find the story entertainin like most other people did; all the men who sat around drinkin with Chris would laugh. Fuchsia looked at me whenever Uncle Chris would tell this story and see that I, like her, wasn't laughing. I didn't find anything about the swamp entertainin either. Maybe I was part of the reason she didn't find the swamp good or a source of stories to be giggled over or have a beer shared over, but instead found the swamp somethin to be avoided—because I hated it whenever the swamp was mentioned, I could feel a rumble start deep in me and I think sometimes she saw it. Sometimes the men who sat around with Uncle Chris would start to tease me, *Hey boy did you get your skirt wet runnin up that swamp when you saw that Lizard Man there, Shit did you squeal like that when that old Lizard Man ripped up your car*, and eventually she just wanted to separate herself from it all. She didn't want to be part of the family. Uncle Chris was an embarrassment and so was I. Her brother.

The only thing that ever took the edge off was getting high with Rudy. Otherwise I couldn't relax and escape. I bought weed whenever I could, I was so scared of runnin out. Dealer amounts of it, I was so intent on stockpilin; but I never did deal. Didn't have that in me.

One time when I was a little kid, I went to Carowinds with Mama, before she died. I saw the big Yogi Bear in Hanna-Barbera Land and ran over to hug it. When I got up close, I saw the mesh hole in the mouth for the person inside to breathe through. I got panicked. "This ain't Yogi!" I yelled. "It's a fake!"

I kicked the giant Yogi Bear and ran around yellin, screamin that it wasn't real, demanding to know where the real Yogi was, and knockin cotton candy displays over. Mama grabbed me and tried to calm me down, and told me, "Honey, there ain't no way you're gonna see the real Yogi Bear, because he ain't real."

I thought of this sometimes when people laughed at me, remembering that I was the one who saw the Lizard Man. I didn't know what to do. I didn't know if I should point out that other people saw it too, which some said they did, or if I should just keep my mouth shut, which I did. Sometimes people wanted me to do things like write a book or go on TV—and Uncle Chris always wanted me to do that stuff, for a price—but I always said no, because I was afraid I'd get made fun of. I saw that movie where that white girl had a bucket of blood get dumped on her at the prom and I was afraid somethin like that would happen to me too, like people would pretend to like me or be nice to me but it would be a fake just to set me up and make fun of me. Plenty of people had made fun of me over the years. I wished sometimes that I could be like that girl in the movie and just fuckin set people on fire. But all I could do was smoke.

People made money off of me and my terror. While I laid awake in bed at nights, sweatin, rollin around in my wet sheets, waking from nightmares if I did sleep, the chamber of commerce planned ways to move traffic from the highways onto Main Street so that the merchants could sell Lizard Man memorabilia. They're all fine to see the mesh mouth.

I was scared. Always scared of the creature that looked at me that night, that tried to tear through Ol' Lucy. Sometimes I wondered if it wanted me, if it was tryin to find me all these years, if it wanted to finish the job that it started. Did it just want the car? Would it go after Rudy? I knew that my own sister was afraid of me, or at least didn't like bein around me. I was fucked up, and I fucked up my family. I let her keep her distance; it was probably better for her.

Rudy came over and we'd get high, and we'd get drunk; we did what we could to keep the Lizard Man away. But it was there, some nights in my dreams, starin at me with those red eyes, comin out of Scape Ore Swamp, crawlin out after me, and some nights I slipped on the rocks and couldn't get out, and the Lizard Man caught me and ate me, sucked my meat off my bones, scraped them with his sharp teeth. Some nights the Lizard Man got me out of the car, tore the roof off, or broke the windshield, and his huge pink mouth suffocated, chewed, swallowed. Sometimes the Lizard Man turned out to be Lindsey, and never said anything, but just destroyed me, tore me apart; and I knew Lindsey was gettin back at me for the times I yelled at her and raised my hands to her all those years ago. The times I called her names. I wished I'd never done that.

Lindsey had left me long ago, so long ago, once things went south for me, and I never found another girl to trust and love, not one who loved me, not one who I didn't want to bash her head in after a while. I couldn't help it.

If Rudy was still at the house and had passed out, he'd wake up from hearin the rustling, the gasping, the yelps, over in my La-Z-Boy, and he'd walk over and wake me up, or toss a throw pillow over at me to wake me.

I'd snap out of it, shift in the recliner, then go back to sleep, tryin to think about something else.

I knew Fuchsia'd always been ashamed of me, embarrassed by the Lizard Man story that followed me. I hated that we weren't closer as a brother and sister should be, but I tried to understand. She didn't like the family. Who would?

But I tried not to think about that as I sat in the house one day with Rudy, Fuchsia, and Uncle Chris, and we watched TV, and for a little while things felt ok because it was a funny program. Uncle Chris was happy because he had a beer in his hand. Fuchsia was curled up ignoring everybody. Rudy was a little high, and he was my best friend, and had always been there for me.

For a moment, I felt somethin like happiness. Maybe it helped that I was kind of high, too, I had gotten a ton of pot, but that all didn't matter now. I felt somethin like freedom.

Then someone kicked down the front door. Someone dressed in all black, head to toe, ski mask, holding a shotgun. Everyone screamed or cursed or gasped or put their hands up. Chris still held onto his beer. The man in black stomped his large feet through the house, to the kitchen counter where all my weed was sitting in the corner, and grabbed it.

I watched the tall figure takin all the weed and shoving it in his pockets.

I was overwhelmed with panic and darkness again.

That is what was inside Yogi Fuckin Bear. That is Lizard Man.
This is the Escaped Whore. This is Me.

The man in black turned to leave, and on his way out I never wanted to be that girl from that movie so bad in all my life. I wanted to lock the door in front of him with my mind. I wanted to dump blood on him, I wanted to set fire to him, to the room, but I couldn't, I couldn't do nothin, couldn't do shit, but I was so angry, all I could do was yell, it all came out of me.

"Fuck you!" It just came out of my lips and I was yellin it at him. He turned and looked at me. "Fuck you!" I yelled it at him again and again, "Fuck you!" I yelled it at him and at Lizard Man and at the man inside Yogi Bear and Lindsey and Uncle Chris' friends and even at Mama.

Everybody started sayin things like *Stop* and *Hush* and *Just go on you got what you want* but he raised his shotgun and shot me in the chest as the others looked on. *No no you didn't have to shoot him What the fuck man Oh my god oh my god We're cursed Holy shit* and the man dressed in black was gone in a second.

They ran over to me. *Call 911* I heard somebody say, maybe it was Uncle Chris. I was hurting, but I smiled because it was all over, and my family was around me, my mama's brother, my best friend, and my sister, and at least I had kept them around in my life, and my sister was over me sayin nice things to me and lookin like she cared about me, and maybe even loved me.

BELOW 1600

Lauren Becker

"The 'demon cat,' which ... allegedly haunts the US Capitol in Washington DC, is said to be an omen of doom for the USA. According to some, the black cat is first seen as a small black kitten, but when approached, it grows to a menacing size."

- Dr. Leo Ruickbie, *A Brief Guide to Ghost Hunting*

The prettier, stupider of the newly-inaugurated President's two daughters loved cats. The smart one loved horses. The smart one, Louise, was allergic to cats, which made the pretty one, Angela, resent her, especially as the only home they had known until now was a horse farm in Virginia. Angela called her sister "Horse Face," which was fairly accurate. Louise didn't mind much. However, as she was also the kinder of the two, she faked injury.

"Dad, tell her to stop calling me that." Louise emulated Angela's whine. Her father, complicit in his daughter's false resistance, said, "You know the horse is a beautiful, majestic animal, Louise. We should all be so lucky as to resemble a horse."

"Fine. Be a horse. Date a stallion. Boys like girls who look like girls," Angela said, frustrated by the exchange, and, as always, hurt and confused by her father's preference of her sister. Her mother liked Angela better, but her father had traded up long ago, and neither the girls nor their stepmother had much interest in getting to know each other. Their mother had developed multiple sclerosis, and moved to a tiny, government subsidized, ADA compliant apartment in New Jersey. It was very depressing to be around her, even for Louise, so they talked to her for a few minutes on Skype on Sundays, and otherwise forgot about her.

Louise was 13 and Angela was 10. Louise wasn't really allergic to cats and wasn't really kind. But she was really smart. Smart enough to fool the President of the United States into making her his favorite, horse face and all. Her goal was to get Angela out of the White House. She had a plan. A detailed plan. A foolproof, detailed, smart plan.

"Hey, Angie. What would you name your cat if you could have one?" Her question was mean, but the expression on her plain face displayed only loving curiosity.

"How many times do I have to tell you, Lou? Jeez. I would have a little girl kitten and her name would be Forsythia and she would be gray and white with big blue eyes like mine."

"That's kind of a hard name for a lot of people to say. Maybe you could call her Cindy." There was a girl who rode their school bus in Virginia whose name was Cindy. She liked to fist fight. Girls or boys. Unfortunately, Angela was one of those girls.

"You're such a bitch, Lou. I'm telling Daddy."

"Who do you think Daddy will believe? Besides, there are lots of nice girls in the world named Cindy and you could name her after them. I guess it doesn't really matter anyways since we can't have cats."

"Well, why do you keep asking me about her, then? I hate you," Angela shouted, running through the enormous house, not knowing where she was going.

They had just moved in two weeks prior. The living quarters of the White House were on the second floor. The President had no trouble finding his way around because nobody ever left him alone. The First Lady knew the way from her bedroom to the limo, so she was fine. Louise and Angie got lost constantly, but the Secret Service found them pretty quickly most of the time, and got them to where they needed to be.

Angela ran downstairs, then walked fast. She did not want to be found and relocated by the Secret Service. Even she knew that the best way to do this was to not act lost. She walked the busy halls, looking for her father. Her walking slowed when she realized how useless it would be to try to make her father believe that Louise was anything other than perfect. Eyes watering, she tried the knob on an unmarked, unfamiliar **door**. The knob turned in her hand, and she opened the **door**. It was not a room. Rather, it was a staircase leading downward. She had found the steps to the White House basement.

Being rather fearless (a quality that often accompanies stupidity), Angela walked down the dark staircase to the basement, which turned out to be complicated underground tunnels. Smug in her knowledge that the place existed, planning to never tell Louise about the door, she explored. It would be her secret place. She found a small alcove, and planned to bring a chair and some candles and cat poster when she came down next. Louise would never find her there, and she could draw pictures of Forsythia and listen to her favorite Taylor Swift song 500 times in a row if she wanted, without being cunningly harassed by her older sister. She found her way upstairs and went to the kitchen for lunch.

Louise was already eating.

"Jeez, you even eat like a horse, Lou. Close your mouth. You're going to make me puke."

Louise continued to display her spaghetti and meatballs. "You know I have problems with my jaw, Angie. You don't have to remind me all the time."

Angela started in on her own plate, not caring about Louise's response. She looked away from her sister's digusting display, staring out the window, thinking of her private place in the basement tunnels.

Later that day, Louise spoke with her father.

"She's getting worse, Daddy. You know I don't mind that much when she calls me names, but it really hurts my feelings when she makes fun of my allergies and my TMJ. I think she's just really unhappy here."

Her father nodded, trusting his daughter, but expecting her, as he did everyone, to provide potential fixes when they spoke to him of problems. "And what do you think is a good solution to your issues with Angela?"

"I was thinking ... it might be a good idea if she went to stay with Mom for awhile. Mom is lonely and she could use some help, and you know she treats Angie like a princess. I bet she would even let Angie get a kitten."

Her father tapped his pen against his bottom lip.

"I'll give it some thought, Louise. Though I wish the two of you would try harder not to fight. My job is very stressful."

"I'll try Daddy." Louise looked miserable. She had been setting up her plan since the primaries.

"OK, honey. Go on back upstairs now. I'll see you for dinner." Louise hugged him and went to her room, satisfied that Angela would be gone soon.

The President considered Louise's argument for a few moments. Her points were sound. He did not have time to play referee, and Angela did seem unhappy. He called his assistant into his office and asked her to connect him to his former wife.

"I have Mrs. Harris on the line," his assistant buzzed in. He cringed a bit, hearing she still used his last name.

The President picked up the phone. "Clare, how are you?"

"I'm fine, Andrew. Congratulations, by the way." Her voice was weaker than he re-called, and he noted some residual bitterness.

"Thank you, Clare. That's awfully nice of you. Listen, I only have a few minutes, but was wondering what you would think about having Angela out for a visit." The custody battle had been unpleasant, and he was fairly certain she would be thrilled.

She didn't answer for a moment. "Why, yes, I would love that. Is she all right? Is Lou-ise all right?"

"They're fine, Clare. The adjustment to the move is taking its toll and they're fighting non-stop. I just thought it might be nice if Angela stayed with you for a while, if you're up to it. Of course, I'll be happy to get you a bigger apartment and pay for her support. I'll have my assistant get her enrolled in school."

Clare paused again, overcome by the offer of exactly what she wanted. She cleared her throat.

"I think that would be just fine, Andrew. Go ahead and make the arrangements. It might be a good idea to get a housekeeper to help me out with her and the upkeep of a larger apartment, as well."

"Of course, Clare. I'll get right on it and let you know when to expect her." He discon-nected the call, problem solved.

◆

Angela had brought her supplies down to the basement alcove, along with some cook-ies and milk. She held a drawing tablet on her lap, sketching Forsythia in different poses. She heard a sound and looked up.

There was a tiny black kitten almost at her feet, green eyes meeting hers. The kitten mewed.

"Hi kitty," Angela said softly, not wanting to scare it. "Where did you come from?"

The kitten mewed again.

"Oh, you sweet kitty. Do you want some milk?" More mewing.

She didn't have a dish, so she poured some milk into her hand. The kitten didn't hesitate. It drank the milk, rough tongue scraping her palm. The kitten was not gray and white, but Angela knew that it was hers, and that Louise couldn't change that, even if she found out about it. When the milk was gone, the kitten stretched out on the floor next to Angela, who lay next to her, stroking the kitten, until they both fell asleep.

She woke to a Secret Service agent shaking her awake, asking if she was all right. She answered that she was fine, and the agent radioed that he had found her in the basement, and would bring her upstairs immediately. She looked around for her kitten, but it was gone.

"So, you got yourself lost, genius?" Louise asked Angela.

"I wasn't lost. I knew exactly where I was."

"And where was that?"

"That's for me to know and you to find out," Angela taunted.

"Well, I know secrets, too," Louise taunted in return. Her father had advised her of Angela's impending extended vacation with their mother.

Angela didn't react, surprising Louise, who said, "Wait until you find out. I'll bet it's bigger than your secret."

No reaction, still. Angela was thinking only of how and when she could get back to the basement and her sweet kitten.

After dinner that night, the President told Angela about her new living arrangements. A few days earlier, she would have been happy to escape Louise.

"No. I'm not going. You can't make me," she shouted at her father.

"Your mother is excited to see you. You can decorate your room however you like, and maybe even get a kitten." He thought this would calm his younger daughter, but she reiterated her refusal.

The President said, "I think you'll be more excited about it when you get there, Angela. You'll leave in three days. Meanwhile, I'm giving a speech honoring teachers tomorrow, and you'll be on stage with your stepmother and Louise. I know you love being on TV."

Angela looked at Louise, who didn't bother trying to hide her triumph. She walked away from the table without responding to either. She had her own plan.

That night, she moved a few things down to the basement, to a space in a different tunnel. The kitten approached, and she picked it up and hugged it. The kitten's purring seemed to hold an answer. She put the kitten down, reluctant, and went back upstairs before she was missed.

The next day, her father gave a speech to hundreds of teachers on the White House lawn. Funding for education had played a key role in his campaign, and the teachers' unions had contributed surprising amounts to help him get elected. He introduced his wife and two children, making the usual references to children being the nation's future, and emphasizing the importance of nurturing them in the present.

When the President turned to leave the podium, a number of gunshots came toward him from different directions. Two bullets hit him. One in the arm, another in his chest. No one else was injured.

The President was taken to the hospital, his ambulance surrounded by police and Secret Service. The bullet to his chest had nicked several veins, leaving him in serious condition.

The girls were not allowed to go to the hospital and were told little. Louise was genuinely distraught and looked to her sister for comfort.

"What if Daddy doesn't make it, Angie?"

"Then I guess we'll both go to live with Mom." She smiled at Louise calmly.

"Are you crazy? Our dad was just shot. Don't you even care?"

"I'm hungry. I'm going to get a snack," Angela stated, knowing Louise wouldn't follow. She headed toward the kitchen. When she was sure Louise wasn't following, she went downstairs to the basement door, down to the tunnels to find her kitten.

Louise did not have a difficult time following Angie, who headed down the steps to the tunnels, calling to the kitten. "Here kitty. Here kitty, kitty. It's me. Angie. Where are you, kitty?

Louise tracked Angela's voice, making note of her own path from the steps. She called to her sister.

"Angie? Angie? You're such a dummy. Is this your stupid secret?"

Angela didn't answer, but Louise felt her approaching.

"Jeez, Angie. Dad is almost dead and you're wandering around some dark tunnels. You're, like, the worst daughter ever."

Then she saw the black cat. Big as her. Green eyes, staring. The giant cat leapt at her. She held her hands in front of her, screaming.

Angela ran to Louise, who was passed out on the floor. She shook her.

"Lou. Wake up. What's wrong with you? Did you fall down? Who's the dummy now?"

Louise opened her eyes, terrified. "The cat."

"What cat? You mean my kitten? You were scared by my tiny little kitten?" Angela laughed.

Louise shook her head, but didn't say more. For the first time ever, she was scared of her sister.

When their father returned to the White House to recover, Louise went to his bed and told him that Angela should stay, especially now. It wouldn't look good to send her away. He needed to have his family around him. He agreed. Nobody had been caught or taken credit for the shooting, and he wanted his daughters close.

"Also, I've been thinking. It's a big house. Angie's been really upset about the shooting. Maybe you should let her have a kitten. I don't mind. Really."

Though a keyed entrance had been added to the basement door, Louise wasn't taking any chances. Angela got her kitten, gray and white with big blue eyes, and forgot the basement and black cat altogether. Louise gave up the pretense of allergies and played nicely with Angela and Forsythia, having concluded that both her sister and cats were smarter and scarier than she had thought.

THE MIDWEST

KANSAS ■ SINK HOLE SAM
Swallowed

INDIANA ▮ MARY WHALES
Bloody Mary

IOWA ■ THE MONSTER TURTLE OF BIG BLUE
The Luckiest Man Alive

SWALLOWED

Gabe Durham

"Legend has it that Inman Lake is the home of a large, snaky lake monster that lives in a portion of the lake known as 'The Big Sinkhole'. Locals have speculated that 'Sam'—as the creature came to be known—'had been living in some prehistoric underground cavern that had somehow filled with water from the sinkhole, allowing him to finally venture forth.'"

- Rob Murphy, *Cryptopia*

When a sinkhole appeared here in Wallace County, Grape Soda's mom hollered for us to watch on TV as sheriff Larry Townsend told CBS News, "Man had nothing to do with this. This is a God thing." We see Larry around town so she was all about it.

"You heard him, boys," she told us. "Time for you to see God's work."

Grape Soda and I were on the laptop watching Yazzie. He was our favorite Minecraft YouTuber for his quick jokes, his playful mods, and especially his earnest enthusiasm for the game itself—the simple and beautiful act of creating. I'm twelve now, four years deep into this hobby, so sometimes I need to borrow Yazzie's love for Minecraft to respark my own. But what Grape Soda's mom meant was get your indoor butts on some bikes and go see where God sank earth.

She sang "This is the Day That the Lord Has Made" at smoke alarm volume till we were out of the trailer. We rode through the park on our Huffys, crossed the tracks by the all-dirt dog park, and rode most of the way on the highway. It's a one-laner with generous shoulder, which didn't keep most drivers from honking at us as they passed. It was hard to tell which wanted us off the road and which were saying hi. From a bike, rage and greetings all kinda sound like danger.

▬

What Grape Soda's mom didn't know was Grape and I had already ridden to the sinkhole twice since yesterday morning when word of it first blew up on Insta.

By the time the news was first telling her about it, we were sinkhole experts, new vocab and all: Beneath the *topsoil*, beneath the *overburden*, acid water dissolves soft rocks slowly over time. With apologies to Sheriff Townsend, that's how it happens. Dissolved rocks create pathways and when it rains, new water flows in, *acidifies*, and then dissolves more rocks. The overburden gets overburdened and collapses, and you've got yourself a *sinkhole*. Aka *shakehole*. Aka *swallow hole*, ha.

What had us all scared was not the sinkhole itself but Sink Hole Sam. Granted, we liked to be scared—we'd been spooked by Dracula, Slender Man, and one weekend Lord Xenu—but we also liked to have some say over when and how the fear takes us. And it had us now. I hated lizards, hated snakes, hated the sandworms in *Beetlejuice*, and the lore around Sam is a trove of triggers.

Sam is a huge scaly lizard with a long Brontosaurus neck and butcher knife teeth. He can subsist on greens but prefers squirrels, raccoons, dogs, and humans. It's said you can hear him coming for you because he begins sucking in early, perhaps even uses that suction to hoover prey right into his wet, waiting mouth. Once he's got you by the feet, he's patient. You can flail, wriggle, and dance, but you're his now, and he'll tear into you as quickly or slowly as he wants.

For the longest time, Sam haunted a series of lakes—the Nessie of murder. It's believed that in this period he consumed over a dozen photographers, that he could sense the particular danger they posed to his freedoms.

But what made Sam truly remarkable in his own right is what happened after all the lakes dried up. Unlike all the soft-skinned other critters in Sam's ecosystem, Sam lived. He somehow found the strength to burrow into the soft earth and made his new home beneath the overburden, popping up only to eat. When a new sinkhole appears coupled with a disappearance, believers say, "There goes Sam."

I know: That's no proof. And believe me, Grape and I had our best men on it.

But in the meantime, there's was a quote I was thinking a lot about. "Millions of dollars have been spent attempting to disprove the existence of Bigfoot and The Loch Ness Monster," notes a fun dumbass article in the *Kansan*—the article that got us into Sam in the first place. "As far as I know, all such attempts have failed, so both creatures must still live, if only in myth." But that last clause was only ass-covering to draw in unbelievers. The idiot beauty of spooky web myths is that the burden is always on the disprover.

On Grape Soda's right bike pedal were the remains of a foot holster that had mostly broken off, so every time he pedaled, there was a fast click-scrape of metal-on-road. The rhythm of it kept his mom's sharp hymn in my head: *This*-is the-day (rest) / *This*-is the-day."

Flat Kansas expanse and then a big dip. That's all the hole looked like.

When we first rode out here yesterday morning, a single friendly patrolman had waved us over and told us not to get too close. When we came back that same evening, a wide zone was taped off and a pair of teenagers made out by the road. Today, after the news hit CBS statewide, the gang was all here. A family of five in white tees ate subs. A woman in a sports bra posed in front of the sinkhole as her much younger boyfriend took photo after photo. Two guys in beards and camelbacks looked to be hiking a full circle around the two-mile-or-so circumference. Here on the highway side of the sinkhole, there was an excited buzz. We were otherwise surrounded by pure dirt desert. I recognized no one.

"This is dumb or whatever," I said, "but I feel like Sam is going to pop out of the ground and suck up everyone here."

"S'not dumb," Grape Soda said as we found a quieter spot away from the Kansas City hole tourists. "What's dumb's thinking Sam'll affect things much when he does." Grape settled in. "Let's say, worst case, Sam exists and last year he ate twenty people. Aw, sad for them, but compare that to all car crashes, all gun deaths, and then all the hot Earth's got in store for Kansas this coming century."

Guess whether this was my first time hearing him talk this way. The big difference between me and Grape Soda was he embraced his smarts and I was too smart to embrace mine. I figured he'd be an ecologist and I'd be a broker. Or whatever the new money-making thing was by then. And while there was no question Grape believed all he was saying, it was also true that Grape got the most abstract when he needed to puff himself up. This was how I learned Grape was scared.

"Think back to a time," he said, "when a single mythical creature like Sam could inspire fear anything near the dread we all carry around with us every day. Shit, how quaint!"

"But this is a local problem," I said. "These are people we know who could die."

Grape Soda did this thing he often did where he twisted the lid off his Nalgene and then flicked the water onto his own face. "You remember that movie we snuck into last year? The teenager who joins a secret squad of British gentlemen?"

"Barely. A scene where...a churchful of racists murder each other?"

"Right. The British gentlemen group up against Samuel L because he's planning to kill off most of the earth's people. It's his last-ditch attempt to curb global warming."

"He talks with a lisp," I said as I remember it. I imagined building an ornate Minecraft desert fortress on the sinkhole, getting an email from Yazzie about it, subject line: *Words don't even...*

"At the end, the British gentlemen kill Samuel L and stop his plan and the movie ends triumphantly—the lead teen even gets to do a hot princess up the butt." I knew where he was going with this now because I knew Grape Soda. "So as the movie high fives itself for a job well done, what's the one thing the British gentlemen don't solve?"

"You want me to say global warming."

"The villain of a shitty retro spy movie is the only film or TV character I've seen who has a serious idea about continuing the species." Watching Grape Soda flinch as he continued to flick water into his own face, he looked a thousand years old. "There's so much bad stuff ahead for all of us—scientifically verified suffering. And still, even now, it's apex predators that give us the real creeps?" he said. " A monster will never be a monster again."

He was fired up so I gave him the last word. *But still*, I wanted to say. *Getting eaten must hurt.*

—

The crowd thinned as the heat doubled down. The camelback hikers continued their slow crawl around the hole, and the cops remained clustered at the entrance chatting with the remaining onlookers. Grape and I passed binocs back and forth, eyes trained on the sinkhole's center, til the moment a little quake sent up a big communal *whoop*— the side of the sinkhole furthest from us sank into the earth and made a portion of the hole's wall fall a bit deeper. One of the caution tape posts fell right in. Apparently this hole wasn't finished.

"Back it up, folks," said a familiar voice. I nudged Grape upon checking out the source. "It's Sheriff Larry," I whispered. "From *TV*."

Talk picked up as we all scooted back from where we were, everybody but Grape, who had the binoculars trained on a little spot of discoloration where the earth sank. He'd been silent, his eyes darting around, clearly having a little conversation with himself in his own head. Grape got up, grabbed his pack, and began to trudge along the edge of the hole to get closer to the new spot. I struggled to catch up, felt the dirt get softer the further we walked away from the crowd and the highway.

We sank into a quiet spell, Grape thinking only of finding Sink Hole Sam, me not wanting to be the one who suggests we turn around. I fixated on the spot where the earth was just a little darker.

In a little-read Sam creepypasta, Sam lures a preteen beneath the sand. All she can see are the scales he's wrapped her in. She notices that within each of the scales are a hundred scales and within those are a hundred more scales, and to see the scales within those scales she shrinks to a hundredth of her original size. One of Sam's scales becomes a sinkhole itself and she falls in. She keeps shrinking until Sam's white blood cells crush her to death, and then she wakes up screaming on the roof of a 76 station. In the story's lone comment, the commenter asked for her three minutes back.

The sun hanged low as we got about 200 yards from the sunk caution tape post. It was about 4:30. I suggested a rest. "You're welcome to," Grape said, not *trying* to be a dick—not thinking of me at all. So I sat, knowing he'd turn soon anyway.

The pure potential of the hole was begging for development. You could build a Minecraft Taj Mahal, a Millennium Falcon, the world's biggest donut! And Yazzie looking at it might go, in his mock-skeever voice, "That's the *second* biggest hole I've ever seen." He's got a name for each of his impressions and that one's called Lenny.

Then I saw where Grape was headed—there was a little cliff where the earth jutted out above the hole, not far from the dark spot. Grape ducked beneath the caution tape, walked up to the peak, and peered down.

The earth shifted beneath him—just a little, just enough.

Grape slid down into the sinkhole. I called out to him. He was laughing. "Woo!" he called back, and tried to trudge back up the hill to me.

But it was harder. The cliff face was steep, and every time he stepped on anything, his handhold or foothold crumbled. Across the hole, people pointed. The pair of camelbacked hikers and a cop walked to our side of the hole, impossibly slowly. Grape continued in vain to climb up to me as the dark Sam spot in the earth sat unmoving beneath him. And then Grape's legs began to sink.

When the hikers arrived, the rope they threw to Grape was way too short to make it down to him. Grape Soda tried to lean forward enough to pancake atop the earth, but his legs were in too deep for that kind of leverage, and the aerobic maneuver seemed to only entangle him further. He was a sitting duck for Sam.

The rescue chopper was in the shop from when an eastern cottonwood branch damaged a blade while the team was rescuing Ms. Martel from her own heart last week, Sheriff Larry explained to us. The nearest working helicopter was currently being negotiated to be flown in from Kansas City—but was on the Missouri side, which complicated things.

An hour passed and the sun dropped. His mom arrived, wept, hummed, waved in the dark. Saddest was when Grape Soda got the sense his struggle made it worse and looked out across the sinkhole to us. He got whiter as the chopper kept not coming.

From here I couldn't even see the thought wrinkles of his smart face. Grape Soda was close enough I could see him, too far for me to yell. Or...does that make sense? I didn't yell, anyway. Instead, I thought, over and over, *My best friend's being eaten but for now he's still here. My best friend's being eaten but for now he's still here.*

Beneath the earth, Sam's long teeth softly tugged at Grape's feet, in Sam's gray eyes a total concentration—the look of a predator who'd already won and was now just tending to logistics. All we could do was watch our own be claimed.

BLOODY MARY

Michael J. Seidlinger

"The story of Bloody Mary, a ghost who appears in a mirror when summoned, has been told many times in countless ways. Depending on the version you hear, its leading character is known by any number of names, including Mary Worth, Mary Johnson, and Mary Lou. But in Indiana, she is known as Mary Whales. According to some, she was a real person who lived—and died—in Lake County.'"

- Mark Meriman et al, *Weird Indiana*

Few faces are beautiful enough to be cast from both sides of a mirror. Ah but here, if you're so privileged to have a look at me, you'll see that I can stand on either side and you, oh you better believe it: You wouldn't be able to look away.

I can already hear their chants...

I could be called upon at any moment, so I must look my best at all times. So popular, so very popular, mhm: They laugh and smile at the thought of my arrival. Oh Mary dearest, how beautiful are you to have known that look of shock in the faces of the many? So well, so well indeed.

The thousands, but which will have my interest?

The perfect face looks as pretty laughing as it does when they scream out in fear. I'm here! I'm here! Beg me to do more than bat my eyelashes. Beg me to be everything they anticipated. The mark of beauty is the call of my name. The color red.

Bloody Mary. Bloody Mary. Bloody Mary.

They would love to see such a perfect beauty as one Mary Worth join them in their clamor, their festivities. Oh, they would, wouldn't they? So sweet and often innocent are their faces until they understand. You join Mary.

Bloody Mary. Bloody Mary. Bloody Mary.

I'm right here, my little ones. Don't stretch out those faces; the worst a frown will do is wear thin their temporary, already fleeting beauty. Let me see that twinkle in their eye. Laughter in candlelight, dearest me, scream out my name.

Bloody Mary. Bloody Mary. Bloody Mary.

So often they are young, barely a single wrinkle or blemish on their porcelain faces. I enjoy the shape of their mouths, the gaze and twinkle of their eyes so beaming it becomes the reason I choose them over the thousands of children that call for me.

Bloody Mary. Bloody Mary. Bloody Mary.

The chatter between their cries is one of wonder, as though they hadn't called on me before. I can see it in their eyes. This one, and that one—they have been privy to this beauty. They have caught my interest. Especially the eldest, the delicate one that does his best to act the most courageous, leading the chant, this so-called game.

Bloody Mary. Bloody Mary. Bloody Mary.

He tells them so many peculiar stories about me, taking the name Worth as royalty as though it hadn't also been Countess, most often written in the diaries of the more fanatical minds.

Mmm, well tell me, what's the mark of my beauty?

Does she break through the mirror? Does she climb out like from some other dimension, pulling people in? Does she claw your eyes out? Does she make you as insane as she is?

Oh dearest, you're so misguided by my myth. How can you command an entire room, much less properly welcome my appearance? Mine has tempted the ages, far beyond any particular fashion.

Bloody Mary. Bloody Mary. Bloody Mary.

Little dearies, don't you know? It isn't the eyes that I take. Mmm, no. I wouldn't dare ruin such young, perfect flesh. Not so much as a single scratch. Oh no, and I wouldn't want to ruin my skin. I'd like to keep every curious gesture as kind and flattering as they were when I finally, oh so wonderfully arrived. I take everything, everything that makes them whole.

Bloody Mary. Bloody Mary. Bloody Mary.

Marvelous watching as they huddle with the lights flickering on and off. The candles, bathed in such a warming glow, only further define how delicate the cut of their flesh, every single cut I would do to you. They love such a grand display. Louder they shout, the more affection I could do without. Won't you show me those teeth?

Are you trying to impress me, hmm?

Bloody Mary. Bloody Mary. Bloody Mary.

How impressive, he is, as he begins his own defense. With the lights off, I gaze upon his costume, what he must assume is me. There are more calling for me on this night than most, the hallowest of eves reduced to candy, costumes, and petty banter. I see the hair, a dark dark black, much like my own. I see the gown, upsetting when I then see the mask adorned.

Bloody Mary. Bloody Mary. Bloody Mary.

In the darkness, their chant drowns this most insulting and shameless display. The blood doesn't course through my veins and neither should it be stained across my face. Not a blemish, no. There shouldn't be. Take every cut and wrinkle from the mask. Remove it all, dear. You should know better than to upset me.

Bloody Mary. Bloody Mary. Bloody Mary.

The lights back on, candlelight drowned by fluorescent glow, their chilling cries turn quickly to laughter. He removes the mask and makes light of everything that makes me who I am. Their chant defunct, replaced with accusations and other banter.

Bloody Mary. Bloody Mary. Bloody Mary.

Just as often, they search for me knowing well that I'll never return their calls. Such curious creatures, they bury the name in the myth, and they leave me disappointed. Oh how could you lead them astray, I ask him. A little tap of the mirror. Once, twice, a third time.

Bloody Mary. Bloody Mary. Bloody Mary.

Did you hear that? A gentle tapping turns into a panicked scraping. Is this what they hoped for? They cannot run from me. The same thought goes through their minds, same as any that might have dared to disbelieve. What was that? Oh my, what could it be?

Bloody Mary. Bloody Mary. Bloody Mary.

The window will not shatter; chatter, their teeth can be heard, the dismay in their faces as they turn and look, seeing not their own reflections but mine. Look, the mirror—the beauty matched by their numbers, four times over, in each shape of their would-be glares, the reflection is entirely mine.

Bloody Mary. Bloody Mary. Bloody Mary.

What youthful faces, and more their reaction when graced by such beauty. See the tears running down their faces. Oh the joy, I would reach out and tear the flesh from their faces. Instead, I bathe in their cries.

Bloody Mary. Bloody Mary. Bloody Mary.

What would you expect upon calling my name? Are you not amazed? Are you not better for having seen my beauty? They call for others, their mothers, fathers, the ones surely they love most. Oh dearies, you have no reason for them any longer.

Bloody Mary. Bloody Mary. Bloody Mary.

Mary is here. Mary is in attendance. Let me feel your flesh. Let me taste those tears. I have no need to pass through when it is them—it is you—that looks first. Now say it with me. Say it with me.

Bloody Mary. Bloody Mary. Bloody Mary.

Now step up onto the counter. That's it. Good little ones. One by one. One by one.

Bloody Mary. Bloody Mary. Bloody Mary.

Yes, now follow his lead. You, smash your head against the glass. Let me see each drop of blood. Let me have a taste. Oh dear, so fresh, so young. Speak of my name, go ahead. Speak it.

Bloody Mary. Bloody Mary. Bloody Mary.

Do you apologize? Oh but you made a mistake. Mmm, but tell me, what is it that you dearies have learned? What makes you think I can believe those words?

Bloody Mary. Bloody Mary. Bloody Mary.

Good. Good. The rest of you, go ahead and feel the glass, the warm warm glass. Your turn now. Join me. Step through the mirror. No. Don't call for mother or father. They would be struck by my beauty. Step through. Join me.

Where you go now is where I watch, letting the thousands yearn to know what it's like to have met me.

THE LUCKIEST MAN ALIVE

Kevin Maloney

"Josh from nearby Cedar Fall, Iowa, claims his 'friend's brother' was horsing around Big Blue with friends as a kid and one friend fell in the pond. Just after the kid walked ashore an enormous serpentine head emerged from the water with mouth agape in an attempt to eat the young boy. Of course the terrified child escaped in the nick of time just like a scene from a good JAWS movie. The children were convinced there was some beast in the pond until later hearing the legend of the Monster Turtle. Simple deduction leads them to believe they encountered the beast himself.'"

- Gene Fitzpatrick, *Hometown Tales*

We were dumbshit kids trying to make our own fun in the horizontal tedium of Iowa. I didn't think about the consequences of my actions. How could I? Every day was a lifetime, totally detached from the day before. One minute I was deflowering my buddy Kyle's little sister, the next I was shooting heroin in a Wendy's bathroom. Then it was Thursday and I seemed to be robbing a Kum & Go with my mom's nylons yanked down over my face to disguise my identity.

What I'm saying is, I was a puppet of boredom. Midwest sadness permeated everything I did, and when that poor girl turned up dead and everybody wanted to know what happened, I couldn't tell them. Not because I was innocent (I wasn't), but because I didn't know the difference between right and wrong. I knew only highs and lows: a brain jacked up on pills and endless fields of nothingness.

I met Martha at the Dairy Queen. That is, I reencountered her in a wild and improbable body. She was working the soft serve machine, moving cones around in little gyrations that spiraled the vanilla upwards and jiggled her backside for the shirtless boys who'd lined up to love her. We were all heartsick, but I had an advantage: I had two misdemeanors and didn't care about my life. A woman picks up on nervousness. You have to approach her with ice in your veins and eternity in your balls. You must be as inevitable as death.

I didn't know she was Frank's little sister. That is, I knew Frank had a sister. I seemed to remember that pigtailed brat sitting in the backseat of Frank's Impala, her incessant whimpering when we forgot about her back there for 3 or 4 hours while we scored some dope and shot it into the gaps between our toes and puked and held each other in the fly-infested kitchen of a prostitute named Nora.

But that summer a miracle happened. Martha's body fat crossed some mysterious threshold. Her ovaries flooded her with chemicals, and suddenly she was a woman with piercing blue eyes and a smile like the Kingdom of God. She hadn't learned to be coy with her new anatomy; her breasts followed her around like puppies without a mother. It gave us all a feverish hunger for dipped cones.

"Hi Snake," she said.

"How the hell do you know my name?" I asked.

"It's me. Martha."

The name meant nothing to me, but she was smiling and standing on her tippy toes, which gave the earth a feeling of abundance that I hadn't felt since I was a child running unsupervised in my uncle Pat's cornfield.

"I want ice cream," I said.

"Soft serve? Blizzard?" she asked.

"I don't know... just make me feel something. Make me feel like a little boy."

She laughed nervously and pulled a cake cone out of the dispenser and began filling it with white cream.

When she handed it to me, I said, "I want to take you out on a date. I have a court hearing next week, and it doesn't look good. There's all this evidence. Fingerprints. Fuck, who would have thought I'd spend ten years in jail because I was too cheap to buy gloves?"

She giggled and gave me her phone number.

It was that easy.

■

I wanted to take her to Big Blue, that cheerless lake sunk in a scraped out garbage can of a quarry, where, for enigmatic reasons, teenage girls' bras popped off like the useless green jackets of budding hydrangeas. But Martha insisted I take her to the high school football game.

I hadn't been back to that madhouse in years. It was as ugly as ever: pregnant cheerleaders, Syphilitic trombone players, guidance counselors ogling the leotard-clad members of the color guard. Even Principal Rivers—a child rapist if there ever was one—sauntering around like a general, his nose painted in the exploding capillaries of his alcoholism.

While Martha stood in line for candy bars and soft drinks, I went to the bathroom and snorted a line of cocaine off the enamel sink as a pimple-faced sophomore stared at my tattoos.

"You're the guy that robbed that old lady," he said.

"She owed me the money," I explained, lighting a cigarette.

"I heard you sold bad acid to Trevor's brother. He jumped off a balcony and broke his neck."

"What do you know about it? The drugs gave him courage. He wanted to die."

I did another line of coke. When I looked up, the kid was trembling. He looked like he wanted to fight. What a bloodbath that would be! I grabbed him by the hair and pushed his head in the toilet and extinguished my cigarette in his ear.

The game was one of those hideous displays of violence that everybody loves because we're all murderers at heart. At one point a housewife implored our linebacker to punch the other team's quarterback in the Adam's apple. Then a dad shouted a nasty remark about their wide receiver's mother, something about raping her. I waited for the backlash from the crowd, but they loved it. They gave him high fives and cheered: "Good idea! We'll all rape her. We'll hold her down and take turns!"

I laughed. It felt good to be among savages. My sins seemed infantile by comparison.

But then the opposing team scored a touchdown and everybody sat down, depressed, and I remembered that these people weren't my friends but regular people who would serve on my jury next week and condemn me to a six-by-six cell for the best years of my life.

"Let's get out of here," I said, grabbing Martha by the wrist.

"I want to see who wins," she complained.

"Nobody wins. Everybody dies at the end."

There was another reason I wanted to take Martha to Big Blue. According to certain friends of mine, mostly acidheads and degenerates, a turtle the size of a Volkswagen Beetle lived in its murky depths. They claimed that if you touched it, nothing bad happened to you for an entire year. Normally I wouldn't have believed a word those lowlifes said, but my lawyer, a real pervert, described my situation as "dire" and suggested I prepare myself for prison life. He said this with his hand on my knee, slowly working his way up to my pecker. This was the man Iowa had offered me by way of a public defender.

"Where are we going?" asked Martha.

"I need some luck," I said.

Martha nodded, squirming in her seat. It was clear she had no idea what she was doing. Only a few years ago she was still serving imaginary tea to a circle of Care Bears.

"Listen," she said. "If we're going to fool around, there's something you should know."

"Don't tell me how old you are," I interrupted. "If you don't say it, it's not a crime."

"I'm on the rag," she said.

"You think I care about that shit?"

Iowa was a devastating place for dreams. Some days the sunset was so pretty I thought I was already dead. Then the drugs wore off and I realized I was standing in the street watching a house burn down, while a frantic mother screamed that her baby was still inside.

Nothing was what it appeared to be.

Nothing good anyway.

We parked in a ditch and stumbled through a cornfield with a flashlight darting this way and that, illuminating freakish green plants whose seeds were 400-year-old gifts from Indians that our ancestors had repaid in smallpox and dead buffalo.

The cocaine made me nervous. I wanted to grit my teeth into powder and be done with those tiny round bones once and for all, but we were almost there and I could smell the swampy love brewing in Martha's pants: muskox with a note of blood. A diamond saw cutting through metal.

We arrived at the quarry but we weren't alone. Bruce Springsteen blasted from a battery-powered radio perched on the fender of a Kawasaki 4-wheeler, on top of which sat a man and woman making love.

"That's called sex," I explained to Martha, pointing.

"I know what sex is," she said.

"We're going to do that in a few minutes. Take notes."

We watched those horny freaks make love. It was terrible. There wasn't any pleasure to be had when it wasn't your body going up and down. They looked like two pigs fighting over an apple.

"I'm going to put an end to this," I said.

I shone the flashlight at the lovers and made a voice like a cop. "You two, don't move! Hands in the air."

The fornicators obeyed.

"You disgust me," I said.

"You're not a cop," said the boy.

"I'm worse than a cop. I'm the angel of death."

The boy laughed. It was Frank. And the girl—my God, it was Sierra. We'd made love on four or five occasions last summer. For a while she was pregnant with my baby, a son. But then we got into a terrible fight, and she drove to Des Moines and paid a doctor to cut my boy out of her and toss his tiny body in an incinerator.

"What are you two doing here?" I asked.

"Fucking," said Frank.

"You beasts."

Frank pulled up his jeans. Sierra lit a cigarette and gave me a poisonous look.

"I want you to meet Martha. My girlfriend." I pointed my flashlight at the corn. Martha stepped forward and gave a tentative wave. Her cheeks were strawberry stains and her braces were wrapped in tiny rubber bands.

"What are you doing here?" asked Frank.

"We were going to screw, but you idiots got here first," I said.

"No. I'm talking to my sister," said Frank.

"Frank... is that you?" asked Martha.

It took me a minute to understand what was happening. Then I saw it. The pigtails quivering in the rearview mirror. Tears and protestations: *You abandoned me, Frank! I'm telling Mom!* And Frank, too strung out to know the difference between yesterday and tomorrow, driving to Dairy Queen to bribe his little sister with a Butterfinger Blizzard.

It was the cycle of our sorrows, the body of Christ lurking everywhere.

Frank paced around in his blue jeans. He kept shaking his head. "Damnit, Snake. Didn't you already screw Kyle's little sister... what's her name?"

"Jenni," said Sierra, taking a venomous puff on her cigarette.

"How do you know that?" asked Frank.

"Snake and I were going to get married until I caught him diddling that little girl."

"I was full of pain," I said.

Frank waved his arms around like he was standing in a swarm of bees. "Goddammit! I'm sick of this shit. You can't fuck my sister, Snake. I won't allow it."

"I'll fuck whoever I want," I said.

"She's fourteen," he said.

"That doesn't change anything."

"If you're dead it changes everything."

"Not really."

There was a time, maybe two or three years ago, when I loved Frank more than my own mother. We did everything together: drink, shit, piss, shoot pool, steal cars and joyride them into lakes. One time we mainlined heroin on a set of train tracks outside of Blue Earth, Minnesota. We fell asleep in one another's arms, only to be awoken by the sound of a freight train thundering toward us at 60 miles an hour. I didn't bother to move. It seemed like a good time to die. To the east, the sky was a soft pink. I thought: that must be what a baby's skin looks like to people who care about other human beings. But at the last second, Frank saved us. He was under the ridiculous impression that it was a good thing to be alive.

None of that mattered now. He reached into his waistband and pulled out a small pistol, a .22.

"Where'd you get the bb-gun?" I asked.

He was trembling. This was the second person in two hours who wanted to do me serious bodily harm. It felt like there would be many more before the night was over.

"I'll kill you, man. I really will," he said.

"I believe you," I said. "But not with that gun."

"Don't fuck with me," he said.

"Leave him alone," cried Martha.

"Shut up!" said Frank. "He's a monster."

Sierra lit another cigarette. The flash of light startled Frank, and the gun exploded in his hand.

"Oh shit," he said.

A puff of smoke rose from the barrel and lingered there in the swampy air. I looked down at my chest. It seemed okay. I tried to take off my shirt to be certain, but my right arm wouldn't move.

"Damn," I said, and sat down. I was feeling extremely light headed. My heart had relocated from my sternum to my shoulder. It was beating furiously, like a tiny jackrabbit was trapped in there.

Frank didn't care. He stepped over my body and ran to his sister, who was also lying down. He tried to prop her up, but she fell back to the earth and hiccupped a gob of blood.

"But I shot Snake!" he complained, apparently, to God.

"It must've ricocheted off my shoulder," I said. "I have extremely hard bones."

It was turning out to be one of those nights where everybody gets shot. I'd been through it before and wasn't anxious to do it again. I didn't mind the bullet so much, but the hospital gives you all these injections. Long needles like kabob skewers that go into your arm and come out the other side.

"I think she's dead," said Frank.

"She's not dead," I laughed. "You can't kill anybody with a .22. It's impossible."

The main thing in these situations is not losing your cool. Nobody ever died from a lousy gun going off. That kind of thing only happened in the movies.

I managed to stand up despite a wild pain in my shoulder that made my eye twitch and caused me to vomit several times. I stumbled over to Martha and had a good look at her. I'd never been so wrong about anything. There was a hole between her eyes, and her mouth hung open like a broken door. She was definitely dead.

"You did it. You killed her," I said.

"No I didn't. I killed you," said Frank.

"But I'm standing here saying things and her face has a hole in it."

Frank tried to protest, but the evidence was right in front of him. Martha lay with her eyes open, stunned by her final vision of this world. In a weird way, she'd never been so pretty. All the blood had drained from her face, except for a trail of it running from her bullet hole.

"We have to help her," said Frank. He tried to lift her, but parts of Martha kept dropping into the mud. It was difficult to watch. During the entire operation, he was talking to her like she was still alive, explaining that everything was going to be okay, that he loved her and was sorry about the time he left her in the Impala when we were mainlining heroin with that crazy prostitute.

Eventually Frank managed to hoist Martha onto the 4-wheeler. He tied her down with some bungee cords and zoomed off into the night.

"Should I drive you to the hospital?" asked Sierra.

"I'm okay," I said.

"But Frank shot you," she said.

"You think I care about a tiny thing like a bullet?"

Sierra shrugged and disappeared into the corn. I walked a few feet and sat down on a rock and became extremely dizzy. I was losing a lot of blood and couldn't make a fist with my right hand, but I wasn't about to take my problems to a hospital; the last time I checked myself into one of those places they got nosy and asked me a bunch of preposterous questions like: *What exactly motivated you to put your fist through a plate glass window?*

Luckily I travelled with medicine. I dug into my cowboy boot and pulled out a length of surgical tubing and a small bag of heroin. I tied off and a fat vein appeared. As the needle entered my arm, a train cried in the distance and a thousand butterflies flew through my belly. Just like that my suffering was an illusion and I was an ear of corn in the hands of an 11-year-old boy standing in the afternoon sun.

Maybe I fell asleep and had an incredible dream, or maybe I was wide-awake and the inky darkness was my black heart slowly taking over the world. Whatever it was, a couple hours later when I came out of my heroin coma, I was covered in blood, and when I tried to breathe my lungs were full of liquid. I struggled to my feet and looked around, but there wasn't any difference whether my eyes were open or closed.

"Hello?" I said. For a minute it was silent, but when I called out again the answer was footsteps.

They say the first time Jesus came to the earth He was peaceful, but the second time His slender arms will be the mandibles of a terrible God. I don't know which visit this was, but when I picked up my flashlight and thumbed the switch, a giant turtle stood before me, tall as a man, its shell like a thousand jeweled belt buckles. The beast took a step forward, then sucked its head and legs inside of itself, leaving only the ornamental casing.

What do you think I did? I reached out and touched it. And just like that my sins were forgiven and the jury said, "Not guilty," and here I am fifteen years later trying to understand why. But of course there's no reason, only endless rows of corn and the world cheering me along as I kill everyone in sight.

THE NORTHEAST

NEW YORK · THE MONTAUK MONSTER
QUESTIONS WITHOUT MEANING

VERMONT · CHAMP
REVISED COUNTERMEASURES

SPENCER

Questions Without Meaning

Bradley Sands

"Twenty-six-year-old Jenna Hewitt of Montauk, Long Island, and three of her friends were walking on the beach on July 12, 2008 when they saw something that startled them: the carcass of a strange beast. Hewitt later told the local newspaper: 'We were looking for a place to it when we saw some people looking at something...we didn't know what it was'."

- Bruce G. Hallenbeck, *Monsters of New York*

The Montauk Monster is upset. His race's entire scouting party consists solely of him, but he has failed at his task. He washed up dead on a Montauk beach. How could this have happened? His species was counting on him to tell them that humans are safe to conquer and eat. Now they are doomed to eat really bland stuff for the next hundred years, and it's all because it's tough to scout for information when you're dead.

The Montauk Monster looks around for someone to answer his questions. He sees many people surrounding him, some aiming cameras and looking curious. "Pardon me," he says to a friendly-looking man, "but can you tell me how I died?"

Local news correspondent Dave Rosenblatt says, "I don't know....but maybe you can help me out. What exactly are you?"

"I am amongst the things that shall push your kind into the abyss, but not before we suck out your scrumptious juices," the Montauk Monster says.

Dave Rosenblatt looks around to see if anyone else noticed what just happened. "Did anyone else see that?"

"See what, David?" his cameraman asks.

"Never mind," he says.

The Montauk Monster is filled with despair. Once again, he has failed to acquire information. He tries to commit suicide, but this isn't in his skill set. "Kill me!" he screams at Dave Rosenblatt, who pretends not to hear him because he's already dead.

REVISED COUNTERMEASURES

Eber Lambert

"Lake Champlain's native monster has been nicknamed, 'Champ'. As first described by Samuel De Champlain, Champ is a serpentine creature, twenty feet long, as thick as a barrel, and with a head like a horse. More recent sightings liken Champ to a long-necked, dinosaur-like predator with paddle-like fins and dark, scaly skin, rather like a cousin of Nessie."

- Charles A. Stansfield, *Haunted Vermont*

"Good morning. I think we can continue now." Martin Basilisk stood at the podium nervously clutching the laser pointer. He nodded to Eve, his pierced and tatted lab assistant at the side the makeshift stage of eight risers. She tapped on her Mac to open Martin's PowerPoint presentation on the large video screen behind and above him. Normally an office-confined policy wonk, today Martin found himself at the podium in Patrick Gym, the focus of national attention in what had become the official situation headquarters on the UVM campus. Like Martin, Burlington, Vermont had also never before been at the epicenter of such a major news event.

The crowd of about 300 people on the floor in front of him was mulling around in a hissing clamor. A cross section of visiting scientists, government officials, major news correspondents, international press, even internet reporters armed with tablets and handheld cameras. Several dozen representatives from nearby town councils and citizen groups were scattered across the bleachers on both sides. Martin pushed his wire rim glasses up the bridge of his nose and adjusted the microphone. Eve tucked her straight black hair behind her ears and gave him a supportive thumbs up.

"Victor gave you the current status and the overall agenda before the break, so I'm going to jump right into my presentation. This is intended to provide a summary of the facts, giving you a brief history explaining how we arrived at the present day situation. It will also provide insight into the criticality of the situation. Then I'll hand things back to Victor to update you on the current state of the region and operations moving forward."

Martin was the Director of Special Projects at the US Department of the Interior. This presentation was the culmination of an investigation he had been leading for the past 18 months.

"After extensive database searches through news articles, legal filings, and state environmental reports, along with some good old fashioned boots-on-the-ground research, we think this all started in the late 1960s. The Essex Junction IBM facility had been in operation for about 10 years. At that time, they used some experimental etchants for integrated circuit fabrication including the carcinogenic compound Tri-ethyl-methanylathene. Production of this compound was banned in 1974. IBM stored approximately 90 barrels of this substance, along with other toxic compounds, in a warehouse across the Winooski River from its facility. This storage building was razed in 1981 with no record of the disposal or relocation of its contents. We suspect that these barrels were surreptitiously dumped into the nearby pond that was located about 100 yards west of this site on the northern property line of a farm owned at that time by Harold Lyons."

Martin spoke at a steady pace, attempting to maintain a calming, serious tone as an old topography map of the Essex Junction area on the screen flipped to a blurry photocopy of a microfiche print out.

"A Williston Town Cryer article from 1976 documents that Harold Lyons lost 26 dairy cattle near the previously mentioned pond in August of that year. The cattle deaths were officially ascribed to natural poisoning. It is believed that Lyons disposed of the carcasses on the east side of the pond, a site he commonly used for agricultural dumping according to a state environmental report from 1980.

'In 1977, Lyons was listed as a plaintiff in the class action lawsuit, Chittenden Farmers Association vs. Apophis Technologies. Although this suit was settled out of court and the record expunged, it is highly likely Mr. Lyons was using the modified bovine growth hormone, Seratonaline, in combination with other anti-biotics used by the dairy industry at that time. Serotonaline was banned in 1978 after it was linked to severe birth defects and mutations in calves, especially when combined with Di-Quino-lone series anti-biotics, which were also later banned for agricultural use. High concentrations of the derivative Serotonacide were reported in organ meat and ligaments of retired dairy cows commonly wholesaled for slaughter for use in secondary meat products. Lyons sold the farm in 1980 to the developers of the Riverside Townhomes which constructed 98 residential duplex units on the property south of the pond."

At this point an increasing majority of the people in the room were fiddling with their phones in otherwise polite silence. Most were more interested in the current news updates rather than the details being presented. Martin paused to look across the audience. His nervousness had dissipated into his normal professorial demeanor. He continued on by clicking his pointer to display a construction planning map of the area near the pond and the housing development.

"In 1984 General Dynamics purchased the property which included the former warehouse site, the pond, and land east of the pond. Their original plan was to drain the pond and surrounding area to reclaim it for expanded construction. While going through the environmental impact process during the permitting phase, they were blocked by the Vermont Environmental Resources department. The agency demarcated the 24-acre swampy perimeter encompassing the pond and declared it protected wetlands. This protected zone was then separated from the main complex by a twenty foot berm topped with an eight foot concrete block wall between the pond area and the rear parking lot of the new manufacturing facility. The entire 70-acres was surrounded by a 10-foot chain link and razor wire security fence on this property line. This fence also enclosed the isolated pond zone on the south, west and north sides. From this point forward, there was no direct access to the pond and adjoining swamp."

A minor disruption flared up backstage as the FEMA lead, Ronin Hyde, and EPA representative, Karl Uberegg engaged in a heated discussion of emphatic whispers and hand gestures. Eve jumped up from her chair at the AV table to restore decorum by herding the two into the locker room behind the stage. Martin paused and reshuffled his notes as their arguing grew louder until the doors were shut behind them. This didn't surprise Martin. The two men had been at odds tactically and strategically for months. Understandably so, since the situation at hand had become quite severe and the remaining options progressively more limited.

Martin attempted to reclaim the rubberneckers in the crowd entertained by the disturbance. The next slide displayed several photos of water snakes on the screen—close up head shots and full body shots showing relative size. This recaptured the attention of many.

"In 1989 the Essex Junction Town News published a story involving two teens killing a large Northern Water Snake -Nerodia Sipendon—measuring nine feet ten inches in length. The location was listed as 'near IBM Road'. Clearly, the only newsworthy reason for such a story was the unusual size of the snake. The average length of a full grown Northern Water Snake is 36-40 inches. This species normally feeds on frogs, salamanders and occasionally small bird eggs or field mice. In this case, however, the boys claimed they found the snake wrapped around and ingesting the carcass of a freshly killed fawn."

This perked up the environmental scientists and zoologists gathered near the credentials table. A cluster of Essex locals in the north bleachers began talking among themselves recalling that story. Among them Leif Russell who was the neighbor of one of the teens back then. The pictures of snakes turned to a present day Google map of the Essex Junction–Williston region. Martin cleared his throat and soldiered on.

"The pond area remained undisturbed for 27 years with the exception of additional contamination. As a result of recently declassified information, we now know that from 2003 to 2010, the southwest wing of the General Dynamics facility was producing a derivative of the Chikungunya virus for potential use in biological weapons. The facility was also reportedly plagued by rats for several years according to janitorial records. Unknown quantities of this viral-active substance and other neural toxins entered indirectly into the pond zone food chain via the dumping of poisoned rodents over the berm by contracted extermination services."

The screen switched from map view to Google Earth view showing the pond wedged between the housing development, the GD facility and the Winooski River.

"In October of 1999, two children last seen playing in the enclosed backyard of unit 87 in the Riverside Townhomes were reported missing. At the time the children were thought to have been taken by their estranged father, possibly taken into Canada. The following February another child from a neighboring backyard also was reported missing though at the time not considered linked to the previous abduction. None of the three children have ever been reported found."

Martin circled both lots with his laser pointer.

"As you can see, both backyards share a boundary with the wooded area abutting the pond zone. Through internet searches and the archives of the Riverside Town homeowners quarterly flyer, from the mid-nineties until 2010 over 31 pets were reported lost. Since 2005, the towns of Essex Junction and Williston have a combined list of 24 missing persons on record, 21 of which are juveniles."

Again the folks from Essex and Williston began talking among themselves. Nearly everyone in that section of the bleachers knew a family with a reported missing person. This anomaly even made national news back in 2010. It used to be a mystery, but not anymore.

"We believe that in this time period the pond water snake population was still moderate, but unlike all other known modern day reptiles, they had developed pack hunting skills rather than subsisting as solitary predators."

The screen display switched to a broader Google Earth view with an overlay of flood regions and arrows pointing west. Martin spoke louder to overcome the increasingly noisy crowd.

"In September of 2011, storms associated with Hurricane Irene flooded the nearby Winooski River. The flood waters encompassed the pond area breaching the low lying section northwest of the pond. It was at this point that the snakes were able to easily migrate into the river and ultimately down into Lake Champlain.

'The first confirmed sighting was near the mouth of the river in June 2012- three snakes on the water surface approximately 20 feet long. Soon after, the US Fish and

Wildlife services captured and killed a smaller snake—16 feet, 8 inches—for analysis. They determined that the snakes had speciated from the Northern Water Snake. The sublingual saliva glands had evolved into venom sacks, and the body scales were now more similar in composition to a plated exoskeleton. The new species was named *Nerodia Rex*—as many of us now know—and was given protected status as an emerging species. The snakes soon were commonly called "Champs" by the locals and regional press, a name given from the fictional Lake Champlain Monster called Champ popularized in the mid 70's. The original Champ was a Loch Ness Monster knock-off made popular as a caricature by the local tourist and novelty trade. Contrary to some stories in the press, Nerodia Rex could not have been the source of any of the alleged Champ sightings in the lake prior to 2011."

Martin displayed a close-up head shot photo of a Champ taken in 2014 with mouth open and fangs extended. This photo had become so commonplace in the media over the last few years there wasn't a gasp of surprise left in anyone in the room.

"In September 2015, Aaron Spear of St. George, Vermont was the first person fined by the Vermont Fish and Game department for killing a Champ. In May of 2016, Jonah Bates of Milton, Vermont was the first confirmed Champ fatality, killed while shore fishing on Compass Point Beach near Mallets Bay. Witnesses provided cell phone video of a large snake estimated at 30 feet in length swallowing Mr. Bates before retreating into the lake."

"It's still on YouTube!" someone from the south bleachers yelled.

A murmur washed across the gym. Martin assumed many in the room had watched the gruesome video. He looked over at Eve, leaning back in her chair, one foot on the table, smirking at him. He had no doubt she had.

"Although still protected, this led to an increase in poaching attempts by local hunters. There have only been two confirmed kills, however, both requiring multiple hits at close range from high caliber rifles. By 2016 the exoskeleton of the Champ had increased in thickness 125% compared to the snake dissected only three years earlier. This makes penetration by bullets under .50 caliber highly unlikely. It was at this point the White House became involved after being contacted by both the US Fish and Wildlife department and Homeland Security. My team at the Department of Interior was then directed to begin this investigation.

'Never before has any scientific organization reported such a hyper-evolutionary progression in a non-microscopic life-form. All anatomical evidence indicates that the rapid development of this species was the result of a unique confluence of additive mutations caused by specific genetic interactions and a unique chemical exposure sequence in a highly homogenous and inbred species over a few dozen generations."

Both CNN and Fox News teams formed huddles near the back of the gym, indicating network had gone to the top of the hour headline recap. NBC and CBS used this opportunity to improve their proximity to the stage for anticipated Q&A by moving into the space the cable guys had abandoned. Martin was ready to launch into some new findings his team had only recently compiled for release. The audience in the bleachers sat tensely silent.

"The primary new spawning ground for the Champs was discovered in May 2017 near Cumberland Head on the New York side of the lake. West Cumberland bay was the site of the now defunct Nature's Way Fresh Water Kelp Farm which operated from 1997 to 2008. The GMO fresh water kelp produced by joint venture between Monsanto Incorporated and Eli Lilly Pharmaceuticals was intended for use as a dietary supplement to promote fertility in farm animals as well as humans. To promote fast and large leaf growth as well as stalk resistance to microbial infestation, the kelp contains grafted whale shark and Kudzu DNA. For an undisclosed reason it also contains a synthetic substance called tetraphenolniacinolaclide.

'For the first few weeks of life, newly spawned Champs feed on minnows and slugs which feed on kelp shoots. This small genetically enhanced food chain has quickly led to a shortened reproduction cycle in Champs as well as continuing to increase in the thickness and impact strength of their exoskeletal scales. More remarkably, they now exhibit a highly accelerated growth rate to adulthood, increasing six-fold. An adult female now spawns approximately every 90 to 120 days and Champs reach full maturity in 8-10 months. The current average adult length is 48 feet with an average girth diameter of 74 inches, 104 inches at the skull. They are fully amphibious and although they prefer water, they can exist on land for several days. They have been clocked at speeds up to 30mph with a lateral slither displacement of less than six feet. Last winter it was discovered that Champs can cocoon prey for extended food storage using gelatinous oral discharge. This allows a cluster of snakes to compress up to a ton of partially digested kill into an ovoidal mass. These are highly evolved and extremely mobile serpents."

At this point Martin had the full investment as well as the suppressed panic and disgust of nearly everyone in the room. His presentation was now describing the horror they had all been reading about and watching in the news over the past months. The crowd remained in a coiled silence as they struggled to digest the facts and data Martin was feeding them. A map of Lake Champlain with colored zones was now projected behind him.

"The normal spring to fall currents and increase in average lake temperature due to global climate change have spread the kelp beds over the past decade. Secondary spawning zones have been identified since spring of 2017 in Shelburne, Converse and Whallon bays and as far south as Bulwagga bay near Crown Point. Our current estimate puts the Champ population density at 10-13 adult Champs per square mile of water surface or approximately 7,000 Champs in Lake Champlain. A doubling of population is expected every 24-30 months. They have been feeding on livestock and human victims extending their hunting ground inland as far as 3 miles. FEMA and Homeland Security have barricaded a half mile back from the shore line in all major lakeside urban areas including here in Burlington, from Colchester to Shelburne. Army and National Guard have been deployed along the barriers with standard issue .60-caliber mounted guns and shoulder-held armor piercing rocket launchers.

'Last June, a significant number of Champs breached the problematic and poorly funded FEMA defenses at the canal in Whitehall and entered the Hudson River. They continue to elude patrols and coast guard offensives. Enhanced barricade zones have been established in Troy, Albany and Poughkeepsie. Dozens of attacks have been reported over the past few weeks, the worst incident being the 12 people killed at a Denny's in Peekskill in August prior to last night's disastrous events in Plattsburg. We believe the defenses here in Burlington are sound but I would like to turn things over to Victor again to detail operations going—"

The rear doors of the gym crashed open. A cacophony of yelling and loud screams exploded into and across the room as people ran in from the lobby. They were followed by black reptile heads pushing through each of the six sets of double doors. Four more creatures emerged from the locker room area behind the stage and slid easily across the bleachers pushing people off and down onto the floor. As snakes entered the gym, more came through the doors behind them. The crowd on the floor quickly became enveloped by an enormous mass of countless writhing serpentine bodies. A pair of heroic CNN cameramen skirted along the south wall to continue live video coverage of the developing tragedy before they too were pulled into the fold of crushed bodies and undulating Champs.

Thrown to the equipment side of the stage by the upended risers, Martin turned and saw Eve signal to him as she began sliding under a riser pushed into the space between the bleachers and back wall. Martin scrambled toward her but was quickly drenched by a paralyzing mix of venom and cocooning mucus.

Lying numb on the floor but still conscious, he listened as the screaming diminished into a sloshing sound. The room grew darker, remaining lit by the video screen overhead displaying Martin's final slide entitled "Revised Countermeasures."

THE WEST

ALASKA • KUSHTAKA
GROWING COLDER

HAWAII • THE MENEHUNE
TROPICAL PARADISE LOST

MONTANA • THE FLATHEAD LAKE MONSTER
SWEET SURRENDER IS ALL
I HAVE LEFT TO GIVE

GROWING COLDER

Janice Lee

"The Kushtaka has been treated in some literature as a boogeyman or hobgoblin. This is inaccurate and does not honor how seriously the Tlingit feel the threat of the Land Otter People. In a sense, the Kushtaka deprived the victim of everlasting life, for his soul could not be reincarnated. The Land Otter lurked to 'save', that is, to capture, those who drowned or who became lost in the woods. The unfortunate captives were taken by the Land Otter People to their homes or dens and, unless rescued by a shaman, were themselves turned into Land Otters."

- Mary Helen Pelton & Jacqueline DiGennaro, *Images of a People*

Tonight it is cold and drunk. Gazed by stars I seize a pitch, light the wick for sleeping. Fingers across hollowed sandstone and Raven whispers in my ear, Time for sleep. Right. Endeavoring. Voice like thundering that whispers and is known when the rolling comes, is formed.

Closes eyes. Opens. To yield to the darkness, there is no difference.

From shore, sounds of water. Eyes fixed on the arriving brightness and already I look to waking up, sunlight and warmth in a moment, not this. Shrinking light, growing cold. I didn't have the right belief and the cold grew larger. Quaking down below.

In the world-sustaining light I remember the warmth of Mother. Black and dark and a face staring down at me. Tiny bristling hairs tickling my lips as I suckled. Sunward following, down behind the lake where it began. Series of bottomless boats. I remember warmth in my mouth and gut and eyes to see her glow staring back at me. Mother's silvery eyes that open, glistened, warmth thrown down upon me. Tiny fulfillments of broken animal skin.

Glints of light later I remember the moment in which I was dying. Surrounded by cold water I didn't struggle. An interruption of explosive beams that shook me but I did not move. I had the wrong belief and so on any given day this could have been the tone of sky under light dimming and every word I uttered drowned before I did. I remember the boat and the last day. Raven whispered silence in my ear and I closed my eyes.

Forgot the growing cold. Just the growing imperious, away. Reconciled in water. There grew the silence and the moon stared down and the warmth in my gut swelled and I was not breathing yet.

I remember I opened my eyes and in the brush I could see the opening to the realm of shadow. A blanket of snow that grew with the cold. Boat overturned and correlation of silence. Lapse of dependence. Spittle on my fingers and bristling hairs above my lips. Mine. In the black I reached, fearing, and fingers grasped. A bird tongue wrapped in a bundle of twigs. My silence. Salt water taste. Steering. Pointed. Cries in the time of hunting, stirring the wind, reverent voices that listen, within.

I remember when I sank. The sun sank to arrive the escaping song and I remembered the tune of Mother. On knees toward the realm of shadow, a visit. Remembering the warmth of Mother. Over there in black the tangles of bristled hair in the trees. Seething. Quivering. Sound of dancing to honor the otter, the one that bridges land and water, life and death.

Shadows dancing and ruddy fire in the center of the many pimply cheeks. One with a thicker forehead. Trooped toes and yellow light. One body standing there. Another shaking its hips like an impulse. Ecstasy was a part of the dance. Shapes of people behind the song.

I made my way to the warmth. I remembered the red heat, its place by a ruddy fire, its place under the struck-down rigid, inherent as home. The place of the belief and suddenly the rattles. A drum beating and knees rattling to perish after the warmth. Not before. Soaked-torn, subdued.

In the heat I followed, though fury tethered and my skin began to boil. How many fingers were rested until the sound met my ears, the awry. Whispers from Raven on the back of my neck. I would not turn my head. Taken. Fallen nature before the warmth. Sounds forming.

Clasped in the arms of warmth there was another one like me. One eye protruding and lips suckling. Mother's bristling hairs on golden, quivering lips. Where Mother used to sit, a different darkness. Declaration of Mother. A different warmth. Declaration of brightness and heat. Warmth in her hands to leverage and in the eyes a growing cold and shadow and a stare that made me want to charge.

Breach of light behind those eyes and so I charged. The vat of cold was boiled from my skin and the other one's crying met my ears, dog tangled with my shins and red fury that was timely met. I bristled with Raven's whispers and the night tones of lowness pushed me further. Taller, thicker, longer. The boiled skin that sleeked into weightless weightiness, a glistening density, fluidity, the growing cold into warmth and because outlying. Themselves. Cleared away.

Mother made wing motions and the point stuck up, black circles where dancing blood clots wrestled with boiled skin. I was tired. Swinging and throwing. When I charged, the other one fell and so I picked her up. Her that looked like me but was cold and hairless. Felt the growing cold and the swift darkness. Dragged her into the light, the orange beacon where stones were thrown and I tasted salty descending. Slowly. Into the warmth of the ruddy whispers and watched her boil.

Mother collapsed and tried to reach out for me but already it was no longer Mother and the round had cycled so the warmth that sprung was only growing cold. And the silence from the bird tongue in my fist, crushed like the vileness of the other one, also thrown into the warmth to boil and now reaching for the cold. I wanted the bliss of growing cold and water. The right belief. Mother screamed for me, pitchwood smell burning and the points all around me but it was for haste that the whispers whispered, The vileness must be cleansed. So it had been done, by my own will, a soul crushed to return the balance. Back to the start. Back anew. The water that dying returns to and long time now, remains. Ha, ha, ha, I thought I heard but I had to turn away from Mother.

Steadily trodding feet and blinding light. Tether-free and bristling hair everywhere. Mother could no longer reach me and would see later the balance returned after a fallen nature. Her warmth would return with another in clergy-justified drumbeats.

Beloved dancing. Rattling. The Mother that would remember and breathe into life.

I was unable to sleep but for a long time it was foggy and I knew I was lucky. I had found the right belief and the growing cold was growing warmth and the itchy place, mishap and boiling, was back there in the snow. I had left behind the silence.

Ha, ha, ha the whisper continued.

Yes, my silence mouthed. Bristling hairs around my lips, the breath: Yes.

Turned sideways and high-pitched whistling far away and in my lips, my gut became cold and ruddy. In the fallen nature I would find the warmth and tomorrow would begin anew but for now I would douse the light and next to the water, sleep.

Tropical Paradise Lost

Gabino Iglesias

*"Some of the most popular Hawaiian myths and legends relate to the
activities of the Menehune, mysterious, Leprechaun-like little people,
the equivalent of the dwarves, pixies, and trolls of other folklore...
Young grade-school children say that their greatest fears are of goats,
tsunamis, and Menhune."*

- John H. Chambers, *Hauaii*

Rebecca was having a very animated conversation with Michelle. Matt looked at them from across the dying fire and smiled to himself. The orange glow from the flames was reflecting off Rebecca's bronzed skin and making her shadow dance on the thick vegetation behind her. It looked to him as if her body was somehow capable of absorbing the fire's energy to keep itself going, making her even more beautiful in the process.

"You wanna hit this again, bro?"

Keith tapped Matt on the right shoulder as if trying to physically ask the question. Matt turned to look at Keith. His disheveled hair and perpetually puffy eyes made him look like a dope fiend. He looked like a cross between a bum and a drunk frat bro and acted like the latter most of the time. Matt wondered for the millionth time why they were such great friends when they had so little in common. Without a word, he plucked the massive joint from his friend's outstretched hand and brought it to his lips.

"You two better leave some of that for me," said Michelle.

Matt looked at her. Her bleached hair, injected lips, and augmented breasts made her look like the kind of woman he'd lusted after most of his life. However, there was something about Rebecca, something other than the grace of her movements, intellect, melodious voice, sense of humor, attitude, and natural beauty of her curves, that made her superior to Michelle in every way imaginable.

"Yeah, and judging by your eyes and smiles, you guys are so high you need to look down to see airplanes," said Rebecca.

The comment wasn't really that funny, but Matt chuckled. Everything about her made him happy, and being on this tropical paradise with her was one of the highlights of their relationship. Moloaa Bay was already behind them and they had no real schedule in mind. They had walked, bathed, smoked, drank, ate, and camped their way down to Anahola Bay. They could go from here to wherever they chose. This freedom meant the four of them were in a fantastic mood, and that sense of general wellbeing was acting as a magnifying glass on Matt's feelings. Without thinking, he handed the joint back to Keith, got up, and started circling the fire to get to the woman he'd been staring at for the previous half hour. The weed was so great it was making his hands feel like balloons, but the only thing he craved at that moment was a kiss from his Rebecca's warm lips.

The rock hit Matt in the chest a few steps before he reached Rebecca.

He looked down at the spot where he'd been hit and then at the two women sitting on the ground a few feet away. They both had smiles on their faces, but their brows had shifted into interrogatory frowns.

The rock hadn't been too big, but it was far from a pebble. Matt looked at Keith. Ruining great moments with stupid comments or silly pranks was just Keith's thing. This time around, though, he wasn't the culprit: he was stretched out on his sleeping bag, one arm serving as a pillow and the other holding the joint to his lips.

"Was...was that a rock?"

Michelle's voice was incredulous.

"I think so."

Matt didn't know what else to say. He was about to take another step forward when a second rock flew out of the darkness in front of him and smacked against his right cheek before he could duck.

"Fuck!"

Rebecca turned around and screamed at the spot where the rock had come from.

"Cut it out! That's not funny!"

Matt rubbed his cheek and looked at his hand. No blood. The weed was making everything mellow and gentle, but he knew he would be hurting a lot more without its help. He gritted his teeth and clenched his fists.

"Come outta there and we'll see if you're man enough to throw another rock!"

"Dude, chill out, there's no one out there. You're just high as a kite."

They all turned to look at Keith. Something about his shaggy hair and honest smile put them at ease.

It was short-lived.

The third rock was much larger than the first two. It flew out of the forest, traced an arc over Rebecca's right shoulder, and hit Michelle in the face. Michelle's head snapped back. She released a sound that was somewhere between a gargle and a scream.

Keith shot up and jumped over the fire before his girlfriend's hands had reached her nose.

Rebecca started pulling her friend up by the elbow.

"Are you okay?"

Michelle groaned. Rebecca knew it was a stupid question, but nothing else came to mind.

"Come out here, you fuck!"

Keith's scream made Rebecca nervous. If they were being attacked, hurtling insults into the trees was probably not the best idea. She kept holding her hands over Michelle's hands.

"Take your hands off and let me take a look!"

Between Keith and her, they helped Michelle stand up. There was blood pouring out of her nose and running down her chin.

"What the fuck, man?"

The chill had been drained out of Keith's voice. His question was a few octaves too high. This prank had gone too far. Thinking that some idiot out there in the dark thought hurting his friends was fun pushed the booze and weed out of his mind and replaced it with indignation and a desire to hurt someone. He took two steps toward the darkness.

"Where the hell are you going?"

He turned to look at Rebecca. She had one hand on Michelle's shoulder and the other on her head. Her eyes reminded him of the way she'd looked the few times they'd had an ugly fight.

"I'm gonna knock this asshole out."

"No, you're not," she replied without hesitation. "You're not fucking running into the forest alone and without a flashlight. Keith, get our flashlights."

Keith caressed his girlfriend's head once more, mumbled something about how everything was going to be okay, and jumped back over the fire. He bent down and started rummaging inside one of the rucksacks that was next to his sleeping bag.

Michelle's wailing had died down. Now she was crying and repeating *fuck* over and over with her hands still pressed against her face. Matt couldn't make out what Rebecca was saying, but she was whispering something into the hurt girl's ear.

"Found them."

Matt reached out and grabbed one of the two flashlights Keith was carrying. He turned it on. A huge yellow circle of light brought the forest in front of him to life. He moved the light around, trying to scour beyond the first layer of vegetation. It wasn't happening. Every time he moved his light, the shadows created by the flashlight made everything behind the first layer look like it was moving.

"We need to go in..."

These assholes needed to be taught a lesson. He was the man to do it. Solving things and defending the weak; those were the things he always did.

"No way," Rebecca interrupted. "You two will not leave us alone here."

Rebecca's tone was ice-cold and bossy. Matt hated when she got that way. He looked at her. Her eyes burrowed into his and squashed any reply that might've been brewing in his brain. A few more seconds passed in silence.

Michelle was looking at the blood on her hands. They all stared at her nose. Blood was still coming, but it didn't seem broken.

"Get her something to clean herself up," Rebecca said looking at Keith. He moved once again as if ordered by a superior. It rubbed Matt the wrong way, but they had a bigger problem to take care of.

"Are we just gonna stand around and wait for these assholes to throw more rocks at us?"

"I think they're gone. We've been pretty quiet and we've heard nothing. Plus, now they know we have flashlights."

She had a point.

Michelle sat back down. The two women stayed together, almost embracing each other.

"I kinda feel like we need to go after whoever did this, but I also kinda feel like staying put is the smart thing...right?" said Keith. He looked like a lost child asking for directions.

"Yeah, we're staying put. Give me your flashlight."

Again, Rebecca's voice was like that of a drill instructor. She had a tendency to take over that Matt hated.

She grabbed the second flashlight and started slowly circling their camp with it, her head tilted to the side to catch any sound. After making two rounds, she sat back down, the flashlight still on and pointing at the forest to her left. Keith broke the tense silence.

"Who the fuck is out there?"

"I don't know," said Matt loudly. "But whoever is gonna get a mouthful of broken teeth when I get my hands on him."

The thick vegetation around them was eerily quiet. The sounds of nocturnal birds were gone. The other strange noises were toned down a bit, as if the whole forest was waiting for whatever came next.

"Do you think it could be the locals?" asked Rebecca.

"Why would the locals come all the way out here in the middle of the night to throw rocks at us?"

"I don't know, Michelle," replied Rebecca. "I don't know why people do the stupid things they do."

"Maybe it could be someone we pissed off on our way here," said Keith. "In some countries they hate tourists even if they haven't done anything wrong."

"Dude, every Hawaiian we've met so far has been incredibly nice," said Matt.

"Any of you familiar with the Menehune?" Rebecca asked.

The question sounded innocent, but Matt knew it was just a way for Rebecca to once again demonstrate how much she knew about the world. He felt as if her PhD in anthropology was something she couldn't leave behind no matter what they did or where they went. The question, he knew, was the start of a lecture.

Only Keith mumbled a no. It was enough for Rebecca.

"They're little people rumored to live in the Hawaiian forests. Legend says…"

"Oh, come on," said Michelle, her voice nasal and carrying the kind of anger that comes from physical pain. "Stop making up crazy campfire stories. We need to…"

"I'm serious," said Rebecca. "Some folks think the Menehune, the little people I'm talking about, were some of the first settlers of Hawaii. They…"

The sound of a twig snapping to the left of their little campsite broke the night and made all of them hold their breath. Both flashlights moved to roughly the same spot in the trees, but the impenetrable darkness stopped them from revealing anything. The silence was once again a wet towel thrown on everything around them.

Keith, frowning, turned to Rebecca. "What were you saying about these little men of the forest?"

"They…people say they came from the tribes that lived in the Marquesas. They stayed here and somehow became very small over a few generations. Then, when the Tahitians came, they were overpowered and had to hide in the forests. They hunt at night. That's the only reason I remembered reading about them somewhere. It's a cool piece of local folk…"

Keith's scream drowned Rebecca's words and made the other three jump. He was signaling to their left and saying something intelligible while taking steps back. They all looked toward the spot he was looking at with bugged-out eyes. Rebecca had to move a bit to look that way, but half of her flashlight's circle still fell on the creature Keith was pointing to.

It stood about two feet tall and looked like it had never taken a shower or had a haircut. His face was covered in dirt and he had a patchy beard. His hair fell down the sides of his head in thick clumps. He snarled at them, his mouth full of yellow, decaying teeth. The move made everyone snap out of their shocked inertia. The two women jumped to their feet. Matt moved next to Rebecca and threw his arm around her waist.

"What the…"

Keith made another noise. This time it was more like a wet snarl. Only Matt turned to look at his friend. In the light of the fire he saw a bloodied stick protruding from Keith's stomach. His hands trembled around the stick, not touching it. Instead, they trembled there. Matt had a hard time processing the images his brain was receiving. Then his friend fell to his knees. A second later, a thick branch flew into the side of Keith's head and knocked him over. Standing behind Keith was a creature just like the one in front of him. His survival instinct kicked in.

"We have to get outta here!"

The two women turned to look at him.

"What…is that?"

Rebecca's curiosity wasn't entirely out of place, but they had no time to deal with it. Matt mentioned Keith's name and pointed toward the slumped body. The creature was now hunched over it, biting into the fallen man's shoulder and ripping chunks of meat off of it.

Michelle screamed, her eyes glued to the flesh hanging from the creature's mouth. The thing before them was moving forward. They took a collective step back. Then something long flew out of the darkness behind the small, filthy being. It struck Michelle in the chest. Matt looked at her. The spear had entered her body right above the heart. He grabbed Rebecca's hand and they immediately started running.

The light of the flashlight was useless. They were just moving away from danger without a plan or a destination. Matt could feel his heart lodged in his throat. He'd never felt fear like this. He felt cold, shaky, and breathless.

His foot caught on something and he went sprawling down, his vice-like grip on Rebecca's hand gone in a second. The flashlight flew out of his other hand, shined on them momentarily as it flipped through the air, and fell to the ground. Rebecca screamed a few feet ahead of him.

"Run!"

He turned around, frantically trying to regain his footing. His body was almost entirely erect when he felt something like a punch to the back of his right leg and heard a crunch. He went down again. Rebecca's labored breathing was further away now. He was getting left behind. Pain exploded in his brain and knocked him back down. He reached back. A spear was lodged deep into his hamstring. He screamed.

Matt dragged himself forward and looked up. The flashlight was illuminating a clear space in the forest. A few small figures were moving toward him. He heard strange laughter. Something like a toddler with emphysema. In the distance, he heard Rebecca scream. The sound carried fear and desperation and squeezed his heart to a full stop for a second. He screamed her name while struggling to move forward. She screamed again, but it was cut short.

A sound came from behind him. A few words in a strange language he'd never heard before. He looked back. It was too dark to see anything.

The second spear hit his left calf. He felt the muscle tear as the rudimentary weapon penetrated his body.

He had to move. He had to make it to the beach. He had to find help. Instead, his good leg remained unresponsive and his arms started shaking violently. Tears started running down his cheeks. That weakness made him mad, made him want to kill those little bastards out there.

Matt's eyes travelled to the place the flashlight was illuminating. The group of creatures was gone. Then the strange laughter came again. This time, it seemed to come from everywhere at once.

Tiny hands grabbed his ankle and pulled his injured leg. Before he could react, more hands darted out of the darkness around him and pinned his arms down. Panic wrapped itself around his chest like a python and squeezed the air out of his lungs.

Suddenly, there was a lot of weight on his stomach. Matt stopped moving his head around, stopped fighting and trying to kick out with his good leg. He looked up. Sitting on him was the first creature they'd seen at the camp. It was snarling like a rabid dog. It came close to Matt's face and said something in the strange language. The stench coming from his rotten teeth made Matt gag.

This one was the first one he was going to kill. Then he would take care of the rest of these midgets and go find Rebecca. They'd find some help at the beach, he was sure of it.

The small beast stood up. Its legs were short, but it managed to keep one foot on either side of Matt. The laughter was increasing in volume, buzzing around Matt's ears like a thousand angry bees.

"I'm gonna fucking kill all of you!"

In response, the being standing over Matt threw his hand out. It came back into his field of vision holding a short stick that had also been sharpened.

One big gulp of air and Matt was going to shake these small fiends off and start dishing out punches. He took half of it before the stick came down and pierced his right eye. His spasms made the laughter grow even louder.

Sweet Surrender is All I Have Left to Give

Robert Vaughan

"Originally spotted in 1889 by passengers aboard the steamer U.S. Grant, the Flathead Lake Monster is described, as many lake monsters are, as being a dark snake or eel-shaped creature that moves through the water in an undulating motion and often appears as multiple humps protruding from the water. The beast has been seen by fishermen, locals and tourists ever since."

- Scott Francis, *Monster Spotter's Guide to North America*

It is steamy mid-July, too hot for boats, the deep lake too cold for skinny dips. So, fishing. I'm touched that Nancy still accompanies me, occasionally sharing a favorite line from her novel. One minute I swat black flies, complain how there are absolutely no biters, how maybe I need to switch my bait to worms instead of lures, when out of nowhere I hear her scream, BRAD! By the time I whip my head around, its tail is wrapped completely around her like baling twine. My last image of her is an open hand outstretched toward me. I dive into the freezing lake. Blackness.

▬

"Finish your Apple Jacks, honey. We'll be late." Avery is doodling on a blank notepad. Seahorses. Dolphins. Tadpoles. Clams.

"Daddy?"

"Hmm?" I look up.

"Did the monster's tail look like this?" She holds the pad toward me.

"Get your backpack." I jump up, snatch her cereal bowl, and it slides from my hands, milk flying everywhere, crashes onto the tiled floor into pieces.

The next spring, I walk along the shore, skipping an occasional stone. No one believes me. Well, maybe Avery.

Four skips. My sister still thinks I'd made it all up. She says Nancy split, joined Fritz in Bozeman.

Six skips. Dad says she was good for nothing anyhow. I step over the rotting trout, its eyes plucked out by a bird of prey.

Eight skips. Like I'd orchestrated it. I stare out across the lake, it's a mirage. Smells like wet felt. The very lake I grew up on. All those campfire stories about bogeymen, about Indians or bears snatching us from our tents. About monsters of the deep.

Avery is sitting in the back, in her own car seat. Something she's done ever since the accident. Flathead Lake is shimmering out our side of the car.

"Daddy can we go swimming this afternoon?"

I shake my head. "Too dangerous, honey. How about Mrs. Hoverman's pool?"

"She stinks like old carpet."

I look in the rear view mirror. "Avery, that's not—"

"Daddy, look!"

I slam on the brakes, steer onto the shoulder. "Stay here." I race to the shore—what was I doing? Strip down to my boxers and dive in.

On gentle autumn nights, most darkening nights when I can't sleep, I go check on my baby girl. If she's sleeping, I sit at the big picture window and watch decaying leaves float onto Flathead Lake, like Nancy and I once did. Searching the surface. Or I'll pop into the bathroom, notice Nancy's facial products arranged just like she had them. Open her creams, smell them, one by one. I'll stare into the mirror until my face becomes someone else. Until I'm looking at a stranger.

SPIDER-MA
McComsey

WORDS OF TERROR

DAVID JAMES KEATON's first collection, *FISH BITES COP! Stories to Bash Authorities* (Comet Press), was named the Short Story Collection of the Year by *This Is Horror*, and his second collection, *Stealing Propeller Hats from the Dead* (PMMP), received a Starred Review from Publishers Weekly. He lives in California.

J DAVID OSBORNE is the author of *Dying World*, *Black Gum*, and *Low Down Death Right Easy*. He runs a small publishing house called Broken River Books. He lives in Portland, OR with his wife and their dog.

GABRIELA SANTIAGO is a graduate of the Clarion Writing Workshop and a proud member of Team Tiny Bonesaw. Her fiction has appeared in *People of Colo(u)r Destroy Science Fiction*, *Betwixt*, *Black Candies*, and the *GlitterShip* podcast. You can find her online at writing-relatedactivities.tumblr.com and @LifeOnEarth89 on Twitter.

RIOS DE LA LUZ is a queer Xicana/Chapina living in Oregon. Her short story collection, *The Pulse Between Dimensions and The Desert* is out now via Ladybox Books. Her work has been featured in *Vol. 1 Brooklyn*, *Entropy*, *The Fem Lit Magazine*, *World Literature Today* and *St. Sucia*.

AMELIA GRAY is the author of four books: *AM/PM*, *Museum of the Weird*, *THREATS*, and *Gutshot*. Her fiction and essays have appeared in *The New Yorker*, the *New York Times*, the *Wall Street Journal*, *Tin House*, and *VICE*. She is winner of the NYPL Young Lion and finalist for the PEN/Faulkner Award for Fiction. She lives in Los Angeles.

JUSTIN HUDNALL received his BFA in playwriting from NYU's Tisch School of the Arts. He currently serves as the Executive Director of So Say We All, a San Diego-based literary arts and education non-profit. He produces and hosts the PRX public radio series *Incoming*, featuring true stories straight from the mouths of America's veterans.

ANDREA KNEELAND is the author of *How to Pose for Hustler* (Civil Coping Mechanisms, 2015) and *The Translations* (Sententia Books, 2015). Her collection of fairy tales, *The Birds & The Beasts*, is forthcoming from Lazy Fascist Press. More of her work can be found at www.andreakneeland.com

JENNIFER D. CORLEY is from the Carolinas but now resides in the even weirder Southern California. She was recently accepted to *Tin House*'s Summer Workshop for short fiction. Current work includes poetry online at *Hobart* and *Queen Mob's Tea House*. Other pieces were included in the Slamdance Film Festival and the book *More Monologues For Women, By Women*.

LAUREN BECKER is editor of *Corium Magazine*. Her work has appeared in *Tin House* (online), *The Los Angeles Review*, *Wigleaf*, *The Rumpus*, *The Best Small Fictions of 2015*, and elsewhere. Her collection of short fiction, *If I Would Leave Myself Behind*, was published by Curbside Splendor in 2014.

GABE DURHAM is the author of a novel called *Fun Camp* and a book about 90s unlicensed Christian video games called *Bible Adventures*. He edits Boss Fight Books and lives in Los Angeles.

MICHAEL J. SEIDLINGER is the author of a number of novels including *Falter Kingdom* and *The Fun We've Had*. He serves as *Electric Literature*'s Book Reviews Editor as well as Publisher-in-Chief of Civil Coping Mechanisms, an indie press specializing in innovative fiction, nonfiction, and poetry. He lives in Brooklyn, NY.

KEVIN MALONEY is the author of *Cult of Loretta* (Lazy Fascist Press, 2015). His writing has appeared in *Hobart*, *Barrelhouse*, and *Vol. 1 Brooklyn*. He lives in Portland, Oregon with his girlfriend and daughter.

BRADLEY SANDS is an author of bizarro fiction. He wrote *Dodgeball High*, *TV Snorted My Brain*, *Rico Slade Will F*cking Kill You*, *Sorry I Ruined Your Orgy*, and other books. Visit him at www.bradleysands.com

EBER LAMBERT grew up in Vermont before moving to San Diego in the early 80's. He writes flash fiction and short essays, and has disowned his bad poetry. He has been published in *A Year in Ink* and some ezines, and he supports So Say We All as a volunteer/contributor and current board member.

JANICE LEE is the author of *KEROTAKIS* (Dog Horn Press, 2010), *Daughter* (Jaded Ibis, 2011), *Damnation* (Penny-Ante Editions, 2013), *Reconsolidation* (Penny-Ante Editions, 2015), and *The Sky Isn't Blue* (Civil Coping Mechanisms, 2016). She is Editor of the *#RECURRENT* series, Assistant Editor at *Fanzine*, and Executive Editor of *Entropy*.

GABINO IGLESIAS is a writer, journalist, and book reviewer currently living in Austin, TX. He is the author of *Gutmouth*, *Hungry Darkness*, and *Zero Saints*. His work has appeared in venues ranging from the *New York Times* to *Electric Literature*. Find him on Twitter at @Gabino_Iglesias

ROBERT VAUGHAN teaches workshops in poetry, fiction, and hike/write. Twice a finalist for the Gertrude Stein Fiction Award. His piece, 'A Box' will appear in the Best Small Fictions 2016 (Queen's Ferry Press). Author of four books: his newest, *RIFT*, is co-authored with Kathy Fish (Unknown Press, 2015). www.robert-vaughan.com

LINCOLN MICHEL is the editor-in-chief of *Electric Literature* and the author of *Upright Beasts*. His fiction has appeared in *Granta*, *Oxford American*, *NOON*, *Tin House*, the *Pushcart Prize* anthology, and elsewhere. You can find him online at lincolnmichel.com and @thelincoln.

ART OF TERROR

ADAM MILLER is a freelance illustrator and professional art guy. Clients include Boston University, Budweiser and Nuclear Blast Records. His work has received recognition from G4TV, the *New York Times* and *Fangoria*. Adam's been published by Terminal Press, Image Comics, and DigBoston among others. He teaches, travels and makes stuff year-round. Instagram: @millerstrations

JACOB CARIGNAN is a New England pop-surrealist. His drawings pull from the natural world around him and the industrial environment of his childhood. His artwork has appeared in several east coast exhibitions and in multiple independent publications. Jacob's currently shifting his focus toward a tattoo apprenticeship and concentrated studio time.

AARON CONLEY is the co-creator of *Sabertooth Swordsman* from Dark Horse Comics and 2014 winner of the prestigious Russ Manning Promising Newcomer Award. Clients include IDW, Boom and Image. Recent artwork can be found in the pages of *Rocket Raccoon & Groot* for Marvel Comics. Aaron currently lives in Florida. invademyprivacy.com

HAIG DEMARJIAN's work spans many media. In addition to relentlessly painting, printmaking and drawing he also co-masterminded the award-winning motion picture *Die You Zombie Bastards!* and created the comic book spin-off *Super Inga*. He is a Professor of Art + Design at Salem State University. www.artofHaig.com, www.SuperIngaSaga.com & follow @PlanetHaig on Instagram.

CORINNE REID is a local to the North Shore of Massachusetts. Influenced by the ambiguous forms of nature, Reid's work brings the subtle beauty of the world to the forefront. Her most recent clients include Penguin Books, *Field & Stream*, Crystal Dynamics, and Gallery Nucleus, among others.

JOSHUA COON is an award-winning marketing professional who currently serves as Director of Content Marketing for Kodak, where he is cohost of the *Kodakery* podcast. He teaches classes in drawing, design, and making comics at the Rochester Institute of Technology, and his work has been featured on *Entropy*.

WILL POTTORFF is a working illustrator and comic artist living in Beverly, MA. A Montserrat College of Art Alumi and gallery operations admin at Martin Lawrence Galleries in Boston, Will continues to create his own brand of independent books and comics showcasing his interests in horror, robots, and the 80's.

PETER PASQUERELLO is an illustrator and fine artist, forever tightrope-walking the fine line between the two. Peter loves so many styles of art that it is impossible for him to decide which style he himself is known for. See his eclectic collection and perhaps you can decide at peterperspective.com.

DEANNA BURKE is a freelance illustrator, and a graduate of Massachusetts College of Art and Design with a BFA in Illustration. She is passionate about the work she does! You are likely to find organic line work and dirty textures in all of her art.

MARIE ENGER is a Missouri-based artist who scratches comics on screens and pads of paper. She drinks obscene amounts of coffee, hangs out with birds, and colors within the lines for a few of your favorite monthly titles. Marie has done work for Image and Dark Horse comics, among others.

PETER BERGAMO JR. spent much of his childhood traveling and making artwork. He would eventually move to the Boston area to focus on illustration at Montserrat College of Art. He has additionally studied abroad in Japan and Italy, an experience that continues to have a profound influence on his work.

DANIEL KERN is a freelance visual artist based in Rockland, Massachusetts. He lives quietly with two cats and a few ghosts, drinks too much coffee and will most likely be buried in a book when he should be working.

CODY VROSH is an artist and illustrator, and the co-founder of Binary Winter Press. He works in a graphic watercolor style, fusing science fiction elements with bold female characters and playful creatures to create a unique brand of speculative pop illustration.

AMANDA BEARD is an award-winning illustrator and designer from Beverly, MA. She received her BFA in Illustration from the Rhode Island School of Design in 2012, and currently balances her time between freelancing and working as a full-time graphic designer for The Home for Little Wanderers in Boston.

VAL TOUKATLY is a Boston-based illustrator, animator, and borderline animal hoarder, whose work has been featured in several publications and gallery exhibitions around the world. Her work focuses on duality and secrets; the hidden and unknown.

SHAEMUS SPENCER is a 3D artist, illustrator, and MFA student in Rochester, New York. Fueled by a love of nonsense and storytelling, Shaemus hopes to make animations and experimental video games after college. You can find him in his studio, on Instagram (@chezmouse), or in your nearest hockey arena.

PAUL LYONS owns and operates the Hidden Fortress Press along the shores of the mighty Woonasquatucket River in Olneyville, Rhode Island, where he draws and prints the most horrible things.

JONATHAN ADRIAN/VENUSJAW is a freelance illustrator based out of central Massachusetts. A geek supreme and nature lover, he is inspired by the works of Arthur Rackham, Mary Blair, Edward Gory, Egon Schielle, Maurice Noble and Jack Kirby. He loves working traditionally in guoache, ink and pencil.

KATHERINE BRANNOCK rotates her time between multiple art disciplines. She's often found slinging ink at Flying Panther Tattoo, or tucked away in her private studio located at San Diego Space 4 Art, where she furiously works on completing her next round of projects for DC Comics and/or La Luz de Jesus Gallery.

SARA RICHARD is an Eisner Award nominated artist currently working with IDW Publishing on ongoing covers for *My Little Pony*. Past credits including *Rick and Morty*, *Bob's Burgers* and the DC Comics *Justice League Tarot Card* set. Sara loves to paint cute things, spooky things and all that lies between.

JIM PONTE (aka Pontman) is a graduate of Montserrat College of Art. He is a spare-time illustrator and a full time sign maker. His work has appeared in several New England galleries and in various independent publications. Jim currently resides in Massachusetts with his wife, Jennifer and Boston Terrier, Cosmo.

BRYCE DAVIDSON lives in Brighton, MA as a freelance illustrator and comic book artist. Growing up Bryce quickly found that drawing was his passion after realizing he wasn't much good at anything else. He attended the Massachusetts College of Art And Design, graduating with a BFA in Illustration. www.brycedavidsonart.com

JEFF McCOMSEY is the Editor in Chief of *FUBAR* and *Mother Russia,* and is a freelance artist carving out a living illustrating funny books and anything else that comes within arm's reach. His work has appeared in various graphic novels, animations, and video games. He currently lives in Pennsylvania with his family.

JOSH MORRISSETTE is a photo-based illustrator living in Central Massachusetts. His art has been seen in galleries throughout New England and in comics such as *Zombie-Bomb!* and *Super Inga*. Josh's photo restoration work was recently featured in the critically acclaimed documentary *Food Fight: Inside the Battle for Market Basket*. facebook.com/jomoillphoto

AFTERWORD

Kudos, careful reader—one complete trip through the States of Terror and not a scratch on you. We threw all the bigfeet, lake monsters, mutants, and demons that this great land has to offer at you, and you still came out on top. Not bad for a first-timer. Or maybe you've encountered them before?

Much like us, our monsters have adapted to changing environs, following us wherever we go. From jungle forest to concrete cities, there's no escaping our crypto-citizens. But maybe, armed with the knowledge gained from our journey, we can ask ourselves, "Are we escaping them or are they escaping us?" and not be afraid to know the answer.

We'd like to thank everyone who helped create this series over the past three years. Our writers and artists devoted their time and skill to help make this project a reality, based on nothing more than the ravings of nutcases who wanted to retell some folk stories. The support we've gained from the people who helped us when we didn't know what we were doing, and the bookstores who took a chance to carry our volumes, has been more than we could hope for.

We'd also like to send our gratitude to the people who originated these stories. Every legend we included, whether it's persisted for a few years or for thousands, taps into a unique part of the collective unconscious that makes the impossible real. While we know their stories will survive for as long as people and dark nights are around, we're happy to have added our twists to these tales. We can't wait to see what future weirdness awaits as time, inevitably, marches forward.

Hm—we may have spoken too soon about you not getting any scratches. Looks like one of the werewolves may have nicked you.

You know what THAT means.

—M.L. & K.M.

RESEARCH OF TERROR

Bastian, Dawn Elaine & Judy K. Mitchell. <u>Handbook of Native American Mythology</u>. ABC-CLIO, 2004.

Chambers, John H. <u>Hawaii</u>. Interlink Books, 2008.

Fairbanks, Randy et al. <u>The Weird Club: The Search for the Jersey Devil</u>. Sterling Publishing Company Inc., 2007.

Fitzpatrick, Gene. "Mason City, IA - The Monster Turtle." <u>Hometown Tales</u>. January 4, 2009.

Francis, Scott. <u>Monster Spotter's Guide to North America</u>. F+W Media, 2007.

Godfrey, Linda S. <u>American Monsters: A History of Monster Lore, Legends, and Sightings in America</u>. TarcherPerigee, 2014.

Hallenbeck, Bruce G. <u>Monsters of New York: Mysterious Creatures in the Empire State</u>. Stackpole Books, 2013.

Marimen, Mark, Troy Taylor, James A. Villis. <u>Weird Indiana: Your Travel Guide to the Hoosier State's Local Legends and Best Kept Secrets</u>. Sterling Publishing Company, 2008.

Martinelli, Patricia A. <u>Haunted Delaware: Ghosts and Strange Phenomena of the First State</u>. Stackpole Books, 2006.

Miles, Jim & Mark Sceurman. <u>Weird Georgia: Your Travel Guide to Georgia's Local Legends and Best Kept Secrets</u>. Sterling Publishing Company, 2006.

Murphy, Rob. "The Legend of Sink Hole Sam!" <u>Cryptopia</u>. June 15, 2010.

Okonowicz, Ed. <u>Monsters of Maryland: Mysterious Creatures in the Old Line State</u>. Stackpole Books, 2012.

Pelton, Mary Helen & Jacqueline DiGennaro. <u>Images of a People: Tlingit Myths and Legends</u>. Libraries Unlimited, 1992.

Ruickbie, Leo. <u>A Brief Guide to Ghost Hunting</u>. Running Press, 2013.

Stansfield, Charles A. <u>Haunted Vermont: Ghosts and Strange Phenomena of the Green Mountain State</u>. Stackpole Books, 2007.

Steiger, Brad. <u>Real Monsters, Gruesome Critters, and Beasts from the Darkside</u>. Visible Ink Press, 2010.

Strait, James, Mark Moran & Mark Scuerman. <u>Weird Missouri: Your Travel Guide to Missouri's Local Legends and Best Kept Secrets</u>. Sterling Publishing Company, 2008.